Look Alive: The Long and the Short of It

Also by John R. Sabine and published by Ginninderra Press
Around the World in Eighty Ways
On Thinking About It
Slam Dunk Poetry (Pocket Poets)

John R. Sabine

Look Alive: The Long and the Short of It

First published 2017 by
Ginninderra Press
PO Box 3461 Port Adelaide 5015
www.ginninderrapress.com.au

Contents

The Meaning of Life

The meaning of life
is ever so simple;
if you don't have a life
then you're not alive.
So – look alive!

Stranger at the Gates

'Are you Smythe, B.S.?' asked the angel, a little brusquely perhaps – you know how it is: rostered duty as sidekick to old St Pete at the gate while awaiting reassignment can be a bit of a drag – 'Smythe with a "y" and an "e"?'

'Er, yes,' replied the newcomer, rather warily, it must be said, 'Benjamin Stanislaus Smythe. That's me.'

'Must be you then. There's a message here for you. Clearly marked, "To be opened before check-in." Here you go.'

Now Benjamin Stanislaus Smythe (Benjamin to his wife, and to himself naturally; Benji to his friends, few though they may have been; Mr Smythe to the rest – when in deference, that is – though just 'BS', or more often 'old BS', even from quite a young age, when in reference; and strangely never, ever just plain Ben) had always tried to do the correct thing, the right and proper thing in every social situation. Necessary, of course, when as a dedicated bureaucrat one inhabited the fringes of the diplomatic ranks and desired, oh so desperately, to work one's way further in. Fussy, some had called him, prissy even, though Benji (let's consider ourselves friends) himself always thought of his attitude more as precise.

Right now, however, if such self-satisfaction were evidence of pride and even such an apparently minor degree of pride were truly a sin, then Benji's secret vanity in his always knowing and doing the correct thing could get him into serious strife. For this was precisely that point in time – if we might be permitted to use that phrase in this rather special in-between temporal situation occupied by the security desk at the Pearly Gates – when sins and digressions weighed very heavily on Benji's mind. As they probably weighed heavily also under Benji's name in the large ledger now being assiduously examined by that same guarding angel.

This was for Benji, of course, as I am sure that it would be for you and me as well, truly a unique situation. In his long and varied career, he had encountered, sometimes in the presence of his beloved wife Madeleine and sometimes not, a wide array of social situations and – as I believe I have already hinted – he could always be relied upon to know exactly how to handle himself. Madeleine would tell him anyway if he did not. Or chastise him, but gently of course, on those rare occasions he had not.

But, as we have already decided, we have here rather a different occasion. Not quite a social situation, I am sure you will agree, and moreover one which few of us have really thought much about, given much consideration to, by way of preparation. I am not sure about you but I had vaguely thought of it as some kind of steadily moving queue, perhaps like sheep (a true biblical analogy, now that you mention it) going through a drafting race, with final chutes to the right or left at the end. Not much chance for debate – that ledger was always up-to-date.

Yet right here, Benji was handed a note, clearly marked as we have said, 'To be opened before check-in.' What was the poor man to do, apart of course from first stepping aside from the queue at security to let the stream of steadily arriving souls pass on by?

If he had been at work – well, actually, he had indeed been at his desk when he…what would be the phrase, 'moved on' perhaps… he might have called Madeleine for some advice. Quietly of course, without making any show of it. Bureaucrats, especially diplomats, even very minor ones, were good at that. But he couldn't see any signs of a phone at the desk and he felt sure that, right here, he was unlikely to be in any regular mobile calling area. Even if he had his trusty BlackBerry with him, which, to his great surprise, he discovered he still did.

But what was that angel doing all this time, if again we can use that possibly inappropriate designator, that Benji was dithering about? Well,

Fred – would you believe it, his name really did turn out to be Fred – while keeping the queue moving and doing the other odd but not very demanding chores required of his (minor) position at the Gates, had also been intrigued by the message for this particular newcomer. He was almost certain that there was no reference to it in the *Manual of Protocol* attached to the heavenly ledger which he had read, hastily, just before he took up his present position. Which, in turn, was in fact just before Benji arrived. So he was as unclear as was Benji regarding the appropriate procedure to be followed but, being a local employee and an angel to boot, he could hardly let this show. The Boss was busy, however, so he would have to handle the situation himself.

But first, if you will permit me, perhaps I should digress a little here in order to address another linguistic anomaly – that is, apart from the business about 'time' that I am sure you have already noticed. I refer of course to Fred and his, well, er, that's the problem, er, gender. I am confident that among themselves they have it all sorted out quite nicely, but when interacting with one of us I'm not sure how angels prefer to be described. Since the only ones I actually know of are, I think, blokes – Michael, Gabriel come to mind, though Gabriel does sound a bit iffy – then just for simplicity can we leave Fred as a he? (Indeed, now that I come to think of it, that demonic Lucifer, Leader of the Angelic Opposition, would almost certainly also have to be male. If anything.)

Of course if you or I had been in Fred's position, I am sure that we would have smartened Benji up immediately, diplomat or not. 'Come on man, hurry up, open the damned note and see what it says. We can't stand around here all day waiting for you to decide what to do.' Fred being Fred, however – you know, an angel and all that, and sort of front-of-house as it were – could hardly be so abrupt. Besides, as we have already discovered, a phrase such as 'all day' would be unlikely to spring readily to his lips, while 'damned' also carries a number of connotations he would probably prefer to avoid.

So Fred waited. And Benji continued to dither.

He turned the note over as he examined it. No envelope, just the folded paper, only loosely sealed and with the bit about opening first written on the outside. Well, no sense in delaying any longer, so Benji drew himself together – as he always tended to do when handling important correspondence – squared his shoulders and slid his finger along the edge to open it out. Nice paper, he thought, official but not too formal. Just the one page. He started to read. Typed. No letterhead. And no date, of course. But you and I had already decided that would have been somewhat superfluous in the circumstances.

'Dear Mr Smythe.'

Well, clearly, it was to be something formal, official perhaps. So he looked next at the signature and for any accompanying title. Always a good idea, certainly useful, as Benji knew from long experience, to establish the identity of one's correspondent before attempting to determine the actual content of said correspondence, formal correspondence that is.

An elegant handwritten signature – Benji, as you might imagine, did so admire good penmanship – but nevertheless one not clearly decipherable, that is, as any name that he immediately recognised. 'Consultor.'

Oh dear, Benji stiffened a little at this. Like any good bureaucrat, even any not-so-good diplomat, he had an inbuilt scepticism of consultants. They always showed up very clearly on his sensitivity radar.

But as he looked again, and in so doing turned slightly to catch a better light, he realised that the author of his mysterious note was a consult*or*, not a consult*ant* as he had at first thought, and although not a familiar title perhaps one less intimidating. That extra light, or possibly just the light from a different angle, then showed up an important feature he had not noticed earlier. There was indeed a letterhead at the top of the page, one of the simple type usually seen (or at least as usually seen by Benji) on inter- or intra-office memos. In very stylish typeface too, that was clear: 'Archives, Previous Records and Future Directives.'

Benji stiffened again. Or perhaps just further. He had started worrying enough about Previous Records, or more specifically worrying about his own previous record, but what was this rather ominous sounding Future Directives? Something from his long-forgotten and long dispensed with (oh dear, again might that also now be another problem?) churchgoing youth suddenly flashed quite unbidden into his mind. Predestination! Even more stiffening.

But he could delay no further. Even Fred, angel and all, was beginning to show a faint touch of restlessness. Benji read on, now with a rush to learn more of his fate – for surely that was what this was all about.

'It has come to our attention...'

Benji halted abruptly. All his training and experience could not allow him to slide glibly over that phrase. 'It has come to our attention', he knew from long experience, he had even used the phrase himself at times, was invariably bureaucratese for the simpler and more direct, 'some bastard has ratted on somebody'. And that somebody more often than not was likely to be you. But what else could he do? He had to read on.

'It has come to our attention that due to circumstances beyond our control' (that is, somebody – somebody else, never me – screwed up) 'your arrival here is, shall we say, for want of any better phrase, somewhat premature.' Good grief. What next? 'If it becomes necessary, or possibly even if you should just so desire, the bearer of this note, our esteemed colleague Fred, could or will, as the case may be' (come on man, get on with it) 'explain to you the circumstances, the most unusual circumstances, I might add, by which you have come to be where you are now. A little ahead of your time, if you will permit my little pun. For you see, Fred was, or maybe – and this is really part of the problem too – still is, your own guardian angel down below.'

So that opening bit about asking Smythe, B.S. his identity was all just a formality. Fred knew who he was all along. And that would also clear up any uncertainty as to why Fred had arrived there only moments before Benji. He had really had to hurry. And of course there would have been no immediate reassignment available either. Quite messy really. Not the smooth and seamless transition one might be led to expect as normal in such circumstances.

'Thus, Mr Smythe, in the circumstances (remember, not my fault at all) we must beg your indulgence.'

Oh no. Indulgence, indulgences, whatever, were something else from Benji's early and – we cannot deny it, certainly not here and now – rather more religious days. Something about time to be spent in some place called purgatory he remembered, which was hardly an appealing prospect, particularly given that current uncertainty about time. And probably now some uncertainty also about 'place'.

'Management' (we can lob any subsequent blame here at least one rung up the hierarchy) 'has decided' (or more likely some anonymous committee finally ended up agreeing) 'that you should be given the choice yourself.'

Benji had always and assiduously avoided making any choices. Was that in the ledger too?

'That is, you may choose to remain here, your ultimate fate yet to be determined in accordance with the facts in your record to date' (we can always claim we stuck to the rules)' or alternatively you can decide to return to take up your former position' (better not to define this too closely)' so that you might be able further to add to or subtract from that record.'

God no, thought Benji. Then immediately thought again. Invoking the deity, even so mildly, might do some more adding or subtracting to his record, surely a hazardous procedure any time and especially so when one isn't too certain of the current balance in that record. And right here and now there was undoubtedly a lot hanging on that balance.

But it seemed he wasn't going to be able to check that balance before making his decision, for the note stopped at that point. With the aforementioned signature, 'Consultor'.

No. There was a short postscript.

'Your answer may be conveyed to Fred, verbally will be sufficient' (gotcha – any catastrophe later we can always claim it was just a simple misunderstanding) 'who will make the necessary arrangements' (now safely out of my hands).

Poor Benji. What was he to do? How could he be expected to cope? Entangled in a bureaucratic mess, no Madeleine to advise him, all eternity – possibly – hanging in the balance. And all that sweet talk in the consultor's note notwithstanding, a decision was obviously required without further delay. Indeed, was required at once, if that look on Fred's face, now that he saw Benji had finished reading, was anything to go by.

The sharp ring of Benji's BlackBerry broke him out of his reverie. He sat up with a start, not quite sure where he had been – or rather where his mind had been – during the past few moments.

His secretary, or let us be more honest and say his shared secretary, came in with a glass of water. 'Rather thought we'd lost you there for a moment, Mr Smythe. You gave us quite a scare.'

Oh yes, his BlackBerry. Caller ID showed up as Madeleine. Strange; she rarely, rarely called him at work, and never late in the afternoon. 'Sorry to disturb you, dear,' she said when he made the connection, 'but I just had the strangest feeling that you might be late. Or something. Do forgive me.'

Or something? Benji shook his head, as if to clear it. Or as if trying to recall something just outside consciousness. 'What the hell happened?' he muttered.

Now you and I know that 'what the hell' might not be the most propitious of phrases for Benji to have used – in the circumstances, shall we say – but that was indeed what came first to mind. And I suspect, though unfortunately we shall never know, that hell (or even just the thought of it as a real possibility) might have been precisely what tipped the balance for Benji in favour of a decision to return to earthly duty.

Benji could always be relied upon to know what to do. Precisely.

The Doctor

Earlier

Arthur was leaving. Not that he hadn't been away before, but this was something special. More permanent perhaps, though if not completely permanent then certainly long-term. Possibly for as much as half as long again as he had already lived.

Arthur was almost twenty. The timing of his leaving was one of the few things, whether matters of family or matters of state, over which his father did not have absolute control. For Arthur was going to Adelaide – well, actually to one of its suburbs, but it was easier and simpler for all concerned just to say Adelaide. For who in Benares had really ever heard of Bedford Park, let alone of its Flinders University? And Petar Naguib was not about to condescend to explain it all to the ignorant. And Flinders University, or more specifically the Flinders University Medical School, had – quite rightly in its eyes – demanded that if Arthur wished to study there, then he should present himself to enrol in the week before classes began, irrespective of when his twentieth birthday might be and certainly regardless of his father's contrary wishes.

Indeed, Petar Naguib had found himself caught, for one of the very few times in his well-ordered life, in something of a cleft stick in this regard. All according to plan – his planning, of course – Arthur's two older brothers were progressing nicely. Winston, or to give him his full name, Winston Jawaharlal Naguib, was already making his mark in the state capital and would soon be making an even greater mark in the state – and eventually national – legislature. Politics was his destiny. The second son, Brunel, was obviously destined (nothing was random with Petar, not even the naming of his sons) to make a lot of money, as well as considerable fame, as an engineer. He too was well on the way.

But what was Arthur's destiny? Or rather, perhaps, what destiny did his father have in mind that naming day nearly twenty years earlier? Well, through his own activities, Petar himself had, even then, commerce and international relations more than adequately covered and the two older boys were there to take care of politics, local and then national, and the country's construction industry. Clearly what was needed beyond that was some lasting legacy, some world-defining humanitarian activity, that would have the family and the Naguib name resonate through the ages. At that time, King Arthur and the whole Camelot scene seemed most appropriate as a model. The details could be filled in later.

Now was later. And this was Petar's present dilemma. Not that Arthur had actually rebelled against his father – that was totally unthinkable – but while agreeing to medicine as the logical starting point for whatever he might want, even need, to do later, he was firmly against studying medicine in England, his namesake and the Round Table not withstanding. This Arthur wanted Australia.

Sometimes quite small things can tip the balance. While Petar was marshalling his thoughts, corralling his arguments, to persuade Arthur to accept the place he had already been offered at the University of London, he happened to strike up what seemed at the time an inconsequential conversation with a little spin bowler in the Australian cricket team then touring India. Petar and one of his innumerable companies had hosted a reception for the team just before the last test.

In the true Irish-Australian tradition of the great spinner Bill 'Tiger' O'Reilly, this young man was not only a superb bowler, he was also a superb talker. Though whether his talking up the whole Australian university scene in general, and Flinders University in particular, where he was then a graduate student, would alone have convinced Petar will forever remain a mystery. What did tip the balance, however, was that over the next five days this Australian bowler completely tied up the

Indian batsmen, especially in the second innings, and virtually won the game, and consequently the series, almost single-handed. Such artistry should not be ignored. His son could go to Bedford Park.

And so Arthur was now leaving.

Then

Arthur was uncertain. Should he leave or should he stay? Perhaps, though, graduation and graduation day, with all its attendant celebrations and excitement, was neither the time nor the place for such a decision. Again, his father Petar's wishes notwithstanding.

Arthur's father was there, of course, flanked and abetted by Arthur's mother, and by his two older and very successful brothers, and by his sister. Was she, too, successful? Hard to say. How does one measure a female's success in a rigidly traditional Indian family? No, she was not married, at least not yet and through no shortage of eligible suitors, and thus also no, she had no children. But she could write, which she did extremely well – and successfully in many people's eyes if not, or at least not yet, in those of her father. And was she also pushing, as were the rest of the family, for Petar's preferred scenario?

With Arthur's passion for both Australia and spin bowling now satisfied – no mean bowler himself, Arthur was a regular in the South Australian second XI, though his dedication to his studies kept him out of the state team – Arthur should now take up where he had left off. Or rather where his father's wishes had left off. Go to England, get a graduate degree, develop a specialty and return to India. Surely that was his destiny. Actually, his sister didn't quite see it that way, but she was wise enough to keep her true feelings well hidden.

And somehow Arthur didn't see it that way either. Well, not just now, not today. Perhaps sometime, some day in the future, but not on this particular day, not at this particular time. Yes, he was still young. Yes, he was intelligent and healthy. And ambitious. And yes, he now possessed a first-class medical degree from a first-class university. But on the day on which he was bestowed that degree by that university, something different called him. Something more, even, though what that more was he was hard pressed to say. And even harder pressed to explain to his disbelieving father and family.

For the more his father pressed upon Arthur the very great medical challenges to be faced in India, the very great heath needs of the Indian people, his people, the more Arthur seemed to be hearing only of the needs of the Naguib family, the challenge of upholding, and by obvious implication of extending, the renown of the Naguib name. His name.

But Arthur could also hear, could also feel, the beat of a different drum. Other challenges, other needs in other places were also calling to him. His spin-bowling friend and mentor from his early days in Australia had retired from first-class cricket, had taken his postgraduate law qualification from Flinders University and gone into legal practice. Not in a big city such as Adelaide, nor even in its suburbs, where his abilities and his contacts would have enabled him to thrive without much effort, but out in the bush, in a small town in the far west of the state, where the going was much tougher and the rewards much harder to achieve. He was a country boy at heart. But those rewards, so often intangible, were also the more satisfying in that they were indeed harder to achieve and where achievement was obtained more by one's own dedication and hard work and less by one's money and connections.

That same challenge appealed also to Arthur. After a compulsory hospital residency, he too went to practice in that same western town. But Arthur was honest. He had to admit that what also appealed to him was the undoubted fact that he had fallen very much in love with his cricketing friend's younger sister and she too preferred the bush to the city.

Now

Arthur was certain. He was staying, not leaving. Petar Naguib might still be right or rather, and more accurately put, he might still want his son to obey his wishes, to fulfil his ideas of destiny. Petar's ideas, that is, not Arthur's.

Oh yes, after those hard-working years spent in general practice in a small country town, anyone could say, as his father did and often, though probably he would have thought of them as wasted as well as spent, that Arthur had earned the right to a better and brighter career. The poor of India still called. And in that call Petar, at least, could claim to discern the call of destiny. Or was it rather just to claim a bigger share of some mythical destiny, some immortality even, for the Naguib name?

Dr Arthur Naguib saw it all very differently. There were poor and deserving in Australia too. And who was to say that they were less, or more, deserving than their Indian counterparts? How do you measure deservedness? Either way, they too deserved his care and attention – and he had given it unstintingly. And the townsfolk, and those in the surrounding countryside served by his practice, all had overwhelmingly welcomed and appreciated this attention. He was loved and his work was recognised by those for whom he cared most, his Australian family and his friends and his patients. The rest of the world could make its own choice.

There was some residual sadness in Arthur's heart, however. His Indian family, or more particularly his father, could not seem to come to grips with, let alone accept, his decision.

But he did have some hopes for a reprieve. And a goal he had set for himself. Perhaps Petar Naguib would finally accept his son's new life for the joy and success that it surely was when he could at last both spell and pronounce correctly his son's new home. Wudinna is really not all that difficult, any more than is Camelot – if one wants to try.

Do Tell Me

Molecular geneticists, I believe they are called. Now that such scientists can determine all of the diseases manifest in one's immediate family tree, they can tell us all so easily what potential disasters we might have inherited. Ah, the marvels of modern medical science! Totally useless for me. I'm adopted.

The Kookaburra's Tale

There is a legend out there in the bush – the Australian bush, that is – and 'tis a wondrous tale to be sure, of the magic to be found in a kookaburra's tail. For when a kookaburra hears of a story told, then that is when it laughs out loud and for ever so long. And each story heard adds one more feather, of its own special colour, to those already there in the kookaburra's tail.

A blue feather means a fun and games yarn, and white of course holds discourse of true love and romance. There are black ones too, for those that are ever so sad, while brown is known for whatever is dark and sombre that the bird may have heard. They are all of them there in the kookaburra's tail.

There are tales from the country, I know, the wide brown land, but some are heard in the city as well. And for sure I can tell, for the kookaburra here in my backyard is both a town and a country bird. I hear him chuckle and chortle in his own special way; he laughs out loud and tells his mates whenever a newly minted yarn appears – and that is when I can see for sure that there's one feather more, clean and pure, right along there in that old bird's tail.

But what happens when, in the course of its day, a feather might fall right out of its tail? When it lies on the ground out there, all cold and all dreary perhaps, is that just all that is left of one great yarn? Now that I cannot concede, for believe you me there's a baby or three in that bird's nest, and from wherever else would have come those colours so true in their little tails?

So there it is and now you know. When a kookaburra sings, it has heard a new song which it passes along to all of its friends. And if that is a bird that you know quite well, then you too will be able to tell, for you will see a new feather, of just the right colour, in that old bird's tail. For all of its stories are held right there, there in the kookaburra's tail.

Old Bob Takes a Leak

I'm sure that Jim Murray (you know Murray's place, up off Wattletree Road) had more than one dog over the years, but I can remember only Bob. Or 'Old Bob' as he always seemed to me. Or 'stupid old Bob', or 'that silly old bugger Bob', as he would most often and most affectionately be described by Jim.

Bob's job was to round up the cows for milking. He might not have been particularly handsome – mostly Queensland heeler (good for the work) and who knows how much of what else – but he did his work quickly, quietly and with a minimum of fuss and bother. Took after Jim in that regard, I suppose.

And he continued to do his job quickly, et cetera, et cetera, even after he lost part of a leg. Left back leg, as I recall, caught in a rabbit trap and then eaten off – again no fuss and bother. He still loped along in his own unhurried fashion, up hill and down, with hardly any discernible difference in gait or action or activity. All, though, with one distinguishing exception. When he needed a leak.

If the territory he wished to mark was on his left, no problem. Lifted his stump and fired away. But on the right was a different matter. As he grew older – and possibly lazier – turning around to shoot was again just too much fuss and bother. So if now he needed to lift his right-side leg, still a necessary prerequisite for pissing, he could do that only by balancing, somewhat precariously, on his two front legs.

Practice made perfect. No circus dog could throw a better arc. But if you were around to observe the performance, then I would have suggested that you best stand five or six feet clear. In such matters, despite his other achievements, Old Bob was not renowned for accuracy.

A Creek By Any Other Name

History does not record whether all that yelling and screaming and running around by a whole pack of young boys actually helped or not. But then again, neither does history actually record that it took three or four – you see, we can't be sure – heaving and sweating men, probably cursing also, first to rope and then to drag that stupid old Jersey bull, vigorously protesting, out of the creek bed. But there are old-timers around who swear that it all really and truly did happen, so who are we to dispute their memories? Not memories, of course, of what in fact they saw happen, but rather just their somewhat vague – you know what old folk are like – recollections of what they were told happened. And it would have to have been by one or more of those kids, who were indeed the only ones they could have consulted. For it all happened, if it happened at all, so much earlier that it is now much too long ago for anyone to be sure. But their recollections are as good as anyone else's explanation. Indeed, better than most, if you ask me.

So given, we all agree, a complete lack of substantial evidence as to the real facts of the matter, let me try to piece together what happened, or could have happened, or might have happened, that cold and blustery day?

Midwinter it certainly was. And probably a weekend, as otherwise those boys should have been at school. No, wait a minute, correct that. It could possibly have been late in the day, and thus any day of the week after school was out.

Almost certainly, the damn bull was Murray's, for he was one of the few cockies now known to have run dairy cattle at the time. His fences then were even worse than his reputation today for having bad fences and losing cattle, though now they are generally in a bit better shape.

Hardly matters now, though, for his descendants have sensibly long given up milking cows to make a living. Anyway, bad fences or not probably didn't matter way back then. The cattle would have needed the creek for water, so it was probably not fenced off anyway. Indeed, there is another long-established story, though probably apocryphal, that that particular creek was one of only two waterways in the whole state not controlled by the government – that is, where the adjoining property holders owned the land right to the middle of the stream and not up to only so far back from the bank. So bloody old Diamond, Murray's bull, would have drunk there anytime he pleased.

So it was winter. So there had been unusually high winds. So an old gum tree had fallen down and blocked the rough beaten track through the creek-bank scrub that the cattle mostly used to get to and from their water. Didn't worry old man Diamond, though; he just bashed his way through wherever he pleased. As he often did.

This time, however, he wasn't quite so smart. It seems that the bank where he chose to go dropped off rather steeply just in from the edge – I did tell you the creek was running a banker at the time, did I not? Thus, inevitably you might say, our friendly neighbourhood bull slipped swiftly into the water. And, when finally discovered, had spent God knows how long vainly thrashing about in a fruitless attempt to extricate himself.

Which makes me think now that the rescue attempt was probably late afternoon after all. Diamond had of course been left behind when the cows had been rounded up for morning milking and his plight had likely gone unnoticed until the cows were again hauled in for evening milking. All the bellowing he must have gone on with during the day wouldn't have made a damn bit of difference; he was far too noisy for his own good at the best of times anyway.

And now, just when the cows needed milking, certainly wasn't the best of times to be attending to a recalcitrant bull. He'd actually done it before – fallen in the creek, that is – but not so much drama had attended his rescue that time. Indeed, he had managed eventually to drag himself out, only some rather agitated cajoling necessary to spur him on. Or out in that case.

No such luck this day. Old man Murray was there, for sure, certainly Curly Jones (no, not the Curly Jones you and I know, but his granddad at least, for there seems to have been one such Jones around forever, and one always close to any excitement but similarly also always ready to lend a hand), probably some ancestor too of Collins, Murray's neighbour across the hill and the only other long-time dairy man in the district (though with better fences, and a superior attitude), an earlier edition of Eades, maybe, from further down the creek, he ran a couple of cows and used the Murray bull, plus of course that gaggle of school kids.

After some PDQ milking, Black Jack (Murray, that is) had brought some strong ropes and Tojo, his ancient plough horse, to do most of the pulling. For much pulling was sure to be needed. But not until after it had taken much weaving and dancing, several attempts and everybody getting soaked to slip a noose around Diamond's misshapen horns and not before the rope had slipped off once, at least, and had broken once or twice. And even then, when all hooked up and ready to go, it took a lot of effort just for Tojo to get a proper foothold further up the bank. That horn rope had slipped at just the wrong time. Someone had also managed to slip a broad noose around Diamond's rump, just below his tail, and it was to this rope that Tojo was connected, while the men pulled at the beast's head. But just as Tojo got a good grip on firmer ground and heaved mightily, one of the men slipped. Collins, I bet. And when he went, they all went.

The whole scene rapidly deteriorated into farce. At that point, all of Tojo's mighty efforts pulling the bull's behind were of more harm than good since the bull's front end, and thus the direction of the pull, could not be controlled. More cursing and more floundering around in the mud to reattach the ropes and for all rescuers, men and horse, again to come to grips, literally, with the situation.

Right. So all ropes are repaired, in place and tight, Tojo and his entourage are all pulling manfully, Diamond still wallowing around but now with the appearance of a little purpose, the crowd cheering, progress about to be made, when… it had to happen. One of the damn kids fell in.

I am sure it would have been Curly Jones who went in after him. He would have been closest to the beast anyway and that is precisely where the kid slipped. Trying to help, I suppose, but way too close for comfort. So all erstwhile productive action stops while Curly does his lifeguard bit. Successfully too, for apart from the youngster's now being sopping wet – who wasn't? – no undue harm seems to have been done to life or limb.

Fortunately the ropes had stayed in place during all of this diversionary excitement, so the rescue operation could continue. And so it did, for another hour or two more, all pulling and heaving, and pushing and whacking from behind too when Diamond was almost out. And out he eventually came but, personally, I think it was eventually all so easy only because a heifer on heat had inadvertently joined the party, upwind, and old Diamond absolutely knew where his priorities lay.

So, after all of that, is there any wonder that everybody in the district agreed that henceforth that hitherto unnamed stream should be forever called Diamond's Creek? Well, not quite forever; the name soon became abbreviated (the Irish always abbreviate everybody's name anyway) to Diamond Creek. Just as we know it today. Though without any surrounding bulls to fall in.

What! You don't believe that this is how Diamond Creek got its name? OK then, give me a better story. And no, I can't tell you why the bull was called Diamond in the first place.

On Cats and Naming Rights

I have heard it said, and I believe it to be true, that whereas dogs have masters, cats have servants. My family and I now seem to have been (faithful, I hope) servants to a wide range of cats over nigh on fifty years.

No doubt the kids would remember the intricate details and proper progression much better than I do but certain characteristics, and certainly some intriguing names, do stick with me. Domper may seem to be an odd name for a cat but not if, as was claimed by someone much more knowledgeable than I (six-year-old daughter probably), she was a cross between a domestic long-hair and a Persian. And she – the cat that is, not the daughter – could be forgiven, or more properly would clearly accept, any such peculiar designation since she was the only one to provide for future generations – five kittens delivered on ten-year-old son's bed. No doubt the mistress of the house providing education on the birds and the bees. And the cats.

And then I suppose that if you are a black cat with four white paws, you would expect, in a normal household, to be called Socks. But if the household is different, like one half American as in our case, then Chicago (as in Chicago White Sox) is clearly much more logical. And then, by the same sort of reasoning, if you are a generally grey cat with just one distinctive white mark on your chest, you might consider Spot logical, but not in this case – the mark was more a Dash than a dot.

Tiger, of course, would seem likely to be quite reasonable. Though not because of its colouring (which I can't quite remember) but because at that time a favourite book with the little ones was *Tiger in the Grass* – of which latter there was plenty, long and in gross over-supply, in our backyard at the time and into which said kitten frequently disappeared.

Later, of course, when the general household reading age increased, so too did the sophistication of our feline nomenclature. Though, after arriving home from some overseas trip, I never did quite fathom why the newly acquired Koshka was named in Russian rather than in English. I suppose, however, that the simple English translation of that word, Cat, wouldn't really have carried as much weight. Or kudos.

Though I can't say that there would be much kudos/clout/prestige/whatever either if you presented with the name Ratbag. But somehow that did seem quite appropriate for such a mischievous kitten. Which kitten, unfortunately, stayed with us for all too short a time – supposedly just wandered off, but we do wonder about our neighbours.

Then you could say also that our final, or at least current, mistress did not do much better than her predecessors in this naming business. At perhaps six months of age, she just arrived. Simply turned up, at first just occasionally, on our back doorstep. Just checking us out for our level of service, I suppose, until we finally abandoned a very firm resolve and did feed her. It seems that she then decided that we were a much more servile lot than her previous mob, so she took us on. A beautiful ginger colour she is, but because of the initially uncertain and possibly only temporary nature of our employ, we never did get round to naming her properly. The kids by then had all left – and with them all formal naming ceremonies – so we seem to have gotten by all these years with just 'the ginger cat'. Naturally it would be way below her dignity to comment. And of course, as did all our feline superiors, she comes when we call, whatever we call, but then only as and when it suits her.

Upper Mitcham

Now Lower Mitcham, of course, that would be quite different. There's something slightly sinister about that name. Something not quite nice could readily happen in Lower Mitcham. One could hardly conceive of such happening in Upper Mitcham. But it did.

Tommy, five going on six, was a cheerful little lad. Healthy, really quite good-looking, always seemed to have handy a happy smile and a cheerful laugh. Friends with everybody. All of which changed. Dramatically. Almost overnight, it seemed. His big brother, whom Tommy adored, took him to the park, behind the sheds, and did something very bad to him.

Tommy's big brother was almost fourteen. Not really grown-up, of course, but at least old enough to have been around the block once or twice. Or so Tommy believed. And that was more than enough for Tommy. His older brother knew just about everything about anything that mattered. And was to be followed and obeyed in all things.

There were two girls in the family between Tommy and his brother. But they were only his sisters, just girls, so they hardly mattered. They could cheerfully be left alone to do their own thing, whatever that might be. So this day Tommy was not about to consult with them, even though they did indeed wonder why he was so excited on coming home after school. But he wouldn't tell. No way. This was between his older brother and himself. And that is why he was excited.

That morning, before they both left for school, different schools, his older brother had told Tommy that when he came home that day he would have something very special in store for Tommy. And that is why Tommy was so excited. And also why the whole sordid business was so disgraceful. It was not just a spontaneous, spur-of-the-moment thing, this callous destruction of Tommy's innocence. No, his brother, his ever-loving and, supposedly, ever-protective brother knew exactly what he was doing. He had planned it all in advance.

So this soul-destroying brother took Tommy to the park. Although took is hardly the right word, for Tommy went along willingly and eagerly. And willingly and eagerly followed his older brother into the bushes behind the old changing sheds. And there it all happened, this hurtful and degrading thing that changed Tommy's life forever. His older brother gave him his first cigarette.

Loudly Flows the Don

Chaos! Catastrophe! The end of civilisation as we know it! Well, perhaps not quite. But almost. Truly, almost. And it all started with a simple, innocuous even, occurrence – a schoolboy asked a question.

Worse still, not just any schoolboy, not even just any Australian schoolboy, but a South Australian schoolboy. Who could imagine that such havoc might arise so simply. No, I admit, it hasn't happened yet, just imminent. Frighteningly imminent.

But he did ask his teacher – and we all know about teachers these days. So what dreadful Pandora's box did he open with his seemingly innocent question?

Be prepared for it. For if he didn't know the answer, what indeed is the world coming to?

'Please, sir,' he asked his teacher, 'who is Don Bradman?'

The Bus

Passengers on the 4.45 bus from the city were little different that day from any other weekday; late shoppers and early-leaving workers mostly, a few tardy schoolchildren and other stragglers. They were on the right bus, just at the wrong time – 4.47, when the bomb exploded.

Two Times Tai Yuan

I really didn't want to go to Tai Yuan anyway! Not even once. So twice in succession could be considered as just a little too much. Too much or not, though, let me give you the details.

But first, I suppose that any English speaker could be forgiven for being a little wary of an airline that boasts the abbreviation CAAC, as did the People's Republic of China's then only a commercial airline. Notwithstanding, if I wanted to fly from Beijing to Yinchuan, as I did, then I would have to CAAC it, or not at all.

Now someone had once told me that for an international traveller there is only one thing more dangerous than flying in China, and that is flying in China at night. Don't you believe them – it can be great fun, as you will soon discover.

But before we get too carried away here, let me give you another relevant piece of useful (or otherwise) information about the friendly skies of CAAC. Booking – in advance, that is – is something of a lottery. You buy your ticket and then you hope – pray even, if so inclined – that you'll win a seat when you front up to fly. And when should you front up? That also has a degree of imprecision, shall we say, quite unknown in the West. Oh, indeed yes, there is an advertised departure time, arrival time too, but if the departure time is something of a gamble, then arriving is even more so. All as my story illustrates.

This day, advertised departure time Beijing for flight CC1207 to Yinchuan (central China, capital of Ningxia province, some two to two and a half hours flying time away) was declared to be 3 p.m. So with the airport maybe no more than thirty minutes by taxi on a good day from my hotel, the Sheraton Great Wall of course, perhaps a 1.30 departure time from said hotel was not unreasonable.

But not reasonably achieved. Much delay doing business downtown that morning, no time for lunch, a quick stop at the Australian Embassy on route to the Sheraton, more business, more unsuccessful attempts to telephone home, rushed packing – and I left at 2.05. Remember 1.30? Not a hope.

But, as they say in the classics, 'not to worry!' The plane was also delayed. So delayed, in fact, that no one at all at Beijing airport seemed now to know just when it was supposed to leave. Or arrive for that matter, as the plane required had not yet come in. 'No time' was the standard reply, seemingly to any question at all about that particular flight – which really meant, I suppose, just that no one was willing to make a guess. Nor was anyone about to bother finding out whether anyone else's guess could possibly be correct.

So I just cheerfully milled around with everybody else, mostly similarly uninformed and similarly would-be passengers like myself. Unlike most of them, however, I was totally oblivious to whatever might have been said – in Chinese – over the airport PA system. But, as with that bit about him waiting and everything coming, we did eventually have a departure time – chocks away at 4.55. What is a mere two hours' delay in the grand scheme of things?

But no departure just yet. Some confusion reigned at the boarding gate – at least for me – as most of the passengers nearby appeared to be bound for someplace called Tai Yuan, not at all like the Yinchuan that I wanted. But, eventually, no panic Dr John, just that this plane stops in Tai Yuan first and in Yinchuan last. So simple.

The problem, of course, was not so simply resolved, for in the event our plane that day stopped in Tai Yuan both first and last. And this is precisely the Tai Yuan where I am now stuck, overnight no less, and where the telling of this tale began.

But at this point, let me back up a little, for I hinted earlier that I had indeed been stuck twice in this same Tai Yuan. And this was now indeed the second time, though actually on the last occasion I had thought for a long time that our halfway point to Yinchuan had been

Xian, but I must have been wrong. I now recognised the Tai Yuan terminal building again.

That earlier story had also begun at Beijing airport. But, would you believe, on that occasion we left exactly on time. Spot on. Or at least we were spot on when we left Beijing for the first time, though not so for the second time. Shall I explain?

As is common at most big international airports if one wants to fly just domestically, and worse if one wants to fly in just some little itty-bitty aircraft and not a you-beaut, whiz-bang Jumbo or one of its similarly sized cousins, one does not score a fancy and enclosed air bridge to walk briefly and serenely from the terminal building onto one's waiting aircraft. No indeed; one is usually hustled surreptitiously down some darkened back stairs, out onto the tarmac, onto a bus (mostly standing room only) and then driven to some point in the distant and faraway reaches of the airport and only there to board said little aircraft. Little, as in required for a flight to Yinchuan.

That time, though, when we arrived to board and depart, there did seem to be a little something more amiss, and it had nothing at all to do with the size of the aircraft. And, what's more, I didn't even have to be able to speak Chinese to know about it. When I had booked my ticket (remember, I told you about booking), I had been assured – and the assurance was repeated at check-in – that I had been very lucky to get a seat. We were full.

But when we took off, we were far from full. Half full, maybe, at most. Never mind, must have been a mistake. Here we were happily and safely up and away, so what was to worry about? At that stage, for me, nothing at all. Though it did seem to me at least a little odd that when we had been gone for no more than fifteen to twenty minutes, we seemed to be approaching a very large city and, moreover, we were also showing every intention of landing there. Even I knew that there was no city of such size so close out. And of course it wasn't another city – it was just Beijing again.

And we were about to land at Beijing airport. Why? Well, just for the simple expedient of picking up the passengers we had left behind the first time. Yes, the bus carrying all those souls needed to make us as full as had been promised had not quite made the distance to the nether regions of the airport before the rest of us had so cheerfully departed. So we went back for them. And so, consequently, not only were we now not on time but we were also late, really late. Late out of Beijing and, of course, similarly late into Tai Yuan.

How late soon became evident when, after all things good and proper seemed to have happened at Tai Yuan to ready us for departure again, we weren't departing. We were just sitting there, in the aircraft, on the ground. Then, ominously for anyone familiar with air travel, we were ushered off the plane and into the terminal. And therein left to do what one always seems to do in any Chinese airport terminal building – just mill around.

Said milling around went on for some thirty, forty minutes, maybe more, before I managed to pick up some clues as to what the problem – there obviously had to be a problem – was all about. The problem was airport landing lights at Yinchuan. Or, rather, the lack of them. Yinchuan airport didn't have any. And it was getting dark – or surely would have been by the time we could reach Yinchuan – and nobody, not even CAAC on a good day, wants to land anywhere in the dark without the benefit of runway landing lights.

I had discovered this critical piece of airline intelligence because the only two foreigners apparently present in the Tai Yuan terminal had eventually and logically gravitated together and the other one, a young Swiss woman, was fluent in Chinese. And, even better, determined enough to make some inquiries as to what was going on. Or wasn't going on.

But the knowledge, while inherently quite informative, was realistically not of much practical use. So we milled around some more – another thirty minutes or so. And, of course, thirty minutes darker. Then, suddenly, much noise, much shouting. These were the sort of shouts that could only be interpreted as 'Come on, hurry up everybody, back on board' or language to similar effect. So we hurried, and/or were hurried, back on board.

But hang on a tick. Let's get this straight. If there weren't any landing lights at Yinchuan an hour ago, there surely aren't any there now. And, moreover, it is now dark even here in Tai Yuan and clearly getting darker still at Yinchuan. Too dark in my book for anyone, including and especially CAAC, to be landing there.

But, never fear, o ye of little faith. All will be revealed. And it was, literally, when we landed safe and sound at Yinchuan in an absolute blaze of lights and glory. But not at Yinchuan commercial airport, at Yinchuan military airport. And all the lights and glory – the runway was lit up like Times Square at Christmas time, with landing lights, searchlights, the whole works – were there primarily not for us at all but rather just for the comfort and safety of a bunch of Chinese jet fighter planes that were practising night manoeuvres. Must have been somebody truly important, other than me of course, on board that flight for us to have scored such VIP treatment.

But all of that was the last time round at Tai Yuan. What about this time? Well, same problem today: runway lights – or rather, again, the lack of runway lights – at Yinchuan airport. Nobody can land there in the dark. And once more it was considered to be too late in the day for us to be leaving Tai Yuan, despite the fact that this time there were at least three good hours of usable daylight left and if someone had got a wriggle on we could have made it easily, only an hour or so of flying time required. But regulations are regulations. Last time it had been winter, so a stop in Tai Yuan had made some sense. Or actually a lot of sense, given CAAC's reputation, even in daylight.

Last time, though, as you learned above, we did leave anyway – and landed in a shower of light at the Yinchuan military airport! But not to be so this time; apparently no one quite important enough on board. Except again for me, of course.

So, eventually, at just after 7 o'clock, some thirty, perhaps forty minutes after it had been decided finally that we were here to stay, we were called to 'Dinner' in the airport café-cum-dining-room. No Chinese banquet, I assure you. But the bed in the nearby airport hotel (as the only foreign devil on board, I was given the only single room available) looked reasonably comfortable and the water was hot enough for a bath. I fully utilised both bed and bath. Though obviously in the reverse order.

So that should have been it. Up, up and away to Yinchuan next morning. End of story. Would that I could have been so lucky.

'Hurry, hurry, we must be at breakfast at 7.30,' said a breathless little old lady with limited English when she poked her head in my room at a mite after 7 a.m. – with me clad only in underpants and shaving cream. So indeed I hurried. So much so that I was in the lobby of the hotel at 7.25. But, surprisingly, on my own. Though, of course, with more clothes and less shaving cream.

Five or so still deserted minutes later, even I was able to realise that all of my fellow passengers, included aforementioned little old lady with limited English, must have gone back to the terminal building for breakfast, some five minutes' walk away and where we had had dinner (did I say dinner?) the previous night. And indeed they had. And at 7.45 (what happened to 7.30? you must be kidding) we had breakfast – again if that is what you could call it.

We had then been told to prepare for an 8.40 departure. How did I know that? Well, in the midst of all of the general milling around at the terminal the night before, I had been befriended by a youngish, prosperous-looking Chinese businessman with impeccable English. As it turned out, he was the European manager (Brussels) for his Chinese firm and was only briefly back in China and had wanted to spend just one full day in Yinchuan anyway. Half his luck, as you might say. But back to my story.

'8.40' my new-found friend said, 'but don't believe a word of it. It is just a nice-sounding, reassuring sort of number – and has no necessary connection with reality.' He did, he really did say that last bit. He knew (knows) China a lot better than I do.

So we didn't believe it – neither of us. Though I can't vouch for anyone else. And come 9, 9.30, as predicted, we still had not left. Our plane was waiting, our pilot was waiting, we were waiting. All geared up and ready to go. And what a beautiful day for flying. Though obviously not for us!

Now – and as they say at the beginning of every tale from Texas – 'You're not going to believe this' (and I'm not sure that I do either, and I was right there) but the message seemed to be that, overnight, two whole cans of orange soda had gone missing from the plane! Shock! Horror! Confusion! Could they possibly have been stolen? Perish the thought! And perish also any thought of our leaving. No way were we about to leave Tai Yuan until a satisfactory explanation was forthcoming. Either the missing valuables had to be returned or the dastardly culprits brought to book before we could even hope to leave.

Oh yes, there were security people at the airport all right, but they were less than useless. A large group had been playing cards when we arrived at the terminal the previous evening and they were still playing cards when we finally left that morning. I think you could have stolen the whole plane, not just its orange juice, and they would have been none the wiser.

But eventually we did indeed leave – actually still minus both the drinks and any explanation, I do believe. At 10 something. Yinchuan by 11.30.

The Perfect Heist

It really was the perfect heist – a small tightly-knit team, each chosen for their specific skills, insider information, impeccable and imaginative planning, precise timing, entry and exit achieved without detection, a clean getaway. Pity, though. At precisely that time all those lovely jewels were someplace else – being valued, I believe.

The Madness of McNaughton

How mad do you have to be to kill someone? No, this isn't just an academic question, some vague sociological theory to be discussed over a good dry red; the court really does need to know. McNaughton certainly killed someone, a dozen people saw him do it. Killed his wife, actually, but that's beside the point. The point is – was he mad (or 'criminally insane' as the law would put it) at the time he did it? Is he still mad?

He was mad at the time all right, 'mad as hell' those same dozen witnesses would say, when he bludgeoned poor Marjorie. Indeed, enough of them have already said so, much earlier in the proceedings, to convince the court and everybody in it. It is now McNaughton's turn in the witness box.

'Raise your right hand and say after me…' The bailiff paused. McNaughton hadn't moved. He tried again. 'Raise your right hand and say after me…'

Still no response. No nothing. McNaughton just looked, stared if you will, straight ahead, with what the newer and more romantically inclined reporters in the court would describe as a dreamy look. Dreamy or not, McNaughton really wasn't looking particularly anywhere. A blank look might describe it best, with an equally blank overall expression on his face. Nothing, just nothing, seemed to be going on behind those eyes. Indeed, if anyone had taken particular notice, you could say that this had been his expression throughout the trial.

The judge got into the act. 'Come on, Mr McNaughton, the court must hear your version of the events on the day your wife died.'

Nothing.

'Come now. Possibly your life, certainly your liberty, are at stake here.'

Still nothing.

And so it stayed for the next three days – in court and out of it. McNaughton remained a complete blank; to judges, lawyers, doctors, family, friends, anybody at all. To all intents and purposes, his mind had completely shut down. Or at least that part of it dealing with rationality. Or sanity.

There was ultimately only one possible verdict. McNaughton is certainly mad now, truly criminally insane; indeed so mad now that we will never know whether or not he was mad when he killed his wife.

So that's how mad you have to be to kill someone. Or, perhaps, just how clever you have to be to get away with it.

A Moral Dilemma

There is a story I should love to tell. Great fiction it would be, with all sorts of engrossing elements: emerging and all-too-strong sexual awareness in a fatherless youth growing up in Melbourne in the mid-1950s, bursting out from a childhood layered with Catholic school (single-sex, naturally; or actually unnaturally) beliefs and all that cumbersome and inhibiting inherent guilt, a conscience riddled with all manner of pseudo-religious guff about masturbation and going blind and so on, all of it too strongly believed (or just too strongly ingrained to be disbelieved), first tentative liaisons with the opposite sex (the fair sex, the pure sex, of course, and thus guilt-free; or assumed to be guilt-free; or not even considered as to whether they might be guilt-free or not; they too were 'Catholic', for heaven's sake; or at least they were at first and mostly, and thus what ecstasy and agony when, later, they were not). And, damn it all, he had to be a premature ejaculator.

There would be a list. 'A' for Anne, 'B' for Barbara, 'C' for Carmel and so on right through the alphabet, with major emphasis upon 'E' and 'K' and 'L' and 'P', 'L' and 'P' especially. And with but few letters missing, for he truly played the field. But that was not unreasonable, nor unusual, nor unacceptable at the time – one date in the 50s did not an item make. Male and female could readily come and go, make and break contact within a wide circle of friends, or several different circles of friends – church, university, sport. But of all the letters, 'P' would feature prominently twice, Pauline right in the beginning and Patricia close to the end. A broken engagement must be as close to an end as one can get.

But no, dear me no, there wouldn't be any scores. Not done, old chap. No numerical scale – no 1 for holding hands through to 10 for 'all the way', that sort of thing – though that was a common scoring system at the time. Perhaps just as well, for in our hero's case it would all have to be very heavily weighted towards the lower end of the scale. Yet even there guilt could still be rampant – that Catholic school admonition again, ringing in his ears, 'Don't get on the train if you don't want to go to the next station!'

Cars, too, would have to feature prominently. How else could one operate successfully? Just getting there and back across a large city in reasonable time was critical, let alone what might or might not have happened when encased together. Encased together, that is, but not actually going anywhere. All the best and darkest spots off the beaten track were well known of course. He would have a friend, whose 'M' was best-friend with his 'L' and who lived way across town from her – well, almost as far away as you could be and still be east and south of the Yarra (Why only there? What, would you go to dinner with someone north of the Yarra? No, I thought not) – and it would be very hard to say how he had managed at all. Must have, though: they would later be married.

But I digress. Our fictional Lothario would not always be blessed with his own transport. Public transport would feature as well, as also long walks home through quiet suburbs in the early hours of the morning. Long periods available for contemplation on the earlier joys of the evening, great opportunities to be consumed with guilt for some of those same joys.

An interesting time, the 1950s, for this story of blossoming sexuality. Not long after the war, shortages of essential supplies really no longer an issue, a huge migrant influx, now no longer almost solely from the British Isles, and coming with them all sorts of different arts, entertainments and customs. And of course pre- the so-called 'sexual liberation' of later in the century, which really means pre-The Pill.

But this would be a story predominantly of Catholic angst, no contraceptives allowed anyway! The Church said so; whether or not God also said so was immaterial. And non-debatable. Even if such things, such unmentionable and undiscussable things, had been readily obtainable at the time, which clearly they weren't, our hero wouldn't/ couldn't even have imagined himself going out and specifically buying a condom. That in itself would be sin enough. So we wouldn't need the threat of an unwanted pregnancy to create any barrier to intimacy. Or too much intimacy. Catholicity was ample enough a barrier. Usually. Hopefully.

This is fiction, remember. Thus your suspension of disbelief would have to allow for such otherwise patent absurdities as at fifteen having to ask in a biology class, 'What is a penis?' all the way through to at twenty-two dating, or at least regularly taking out, one special girl (the aforesaid 'L') for well over a year before ever asking for a goodnight kiss. Which of course frustrated her no end, he would later find out from a mutual friend. Indeed, that same 'M' mentioned above.

Just think of the indelicacies that could be covered by such a story. Of course mostly just necking (necking – I haven't heard that word for years) but even so overlaid with all sorts of adolescent fumbling attempts to go somewhere further. Below the neck, I suppose you would have to say. And in the process progressively learning more and more about the intricacies of female apparel – where the key buttons and clasps and snaps and hooks and eyes might be located and what might be the most dexterous method for releasing them while still otherwise entangled and engaged.

And all activity, legit or not, suddenly cut off when – bang! Ejaculation. Premature. Every damn time, or so it seemed. The train had duly arrived at the next station. What any of the A to Z line-up might have thought of that sudden cessation of vigorous activity was never determined. Who knows – perhaps they were on the same train?

So, get ready for some sizzling fiction. Except, except, damn it all again, I can't. For it all happens to be true! And no good little Catholic boy of the 1950s would ever, could ever, reveal such activities. Would he? Could he? For that might implicate otherwise innocent (innocent?) parties. Guilt still rides supreme.

The Chronicles of Pericles

(Perhaps the greatest literary discovery of all time)

Introduction

It seems only now, but even now only slowly and spasmodically, that the true story of the *Chronicles of Pericles*, initially claimed to be the greatest literary find of the millennium, is coming to light. Thus, despite the very best efforts of the Greek Department of Antiquities to keep a tight rein on all information relevant to this astounding discovery, it would appear that certain pertinent facts can be held as legitimately revealed. These relate primarily to the three crucial issues to be discussed in this present introductory paper, namely the manner of the discovery of the *Chronicles* (a series of ancient manuscripts), the physical nature of the manuscripts themselves and the general characteristics of the language used in them and of the stories told there. An initial translation of the first document found, Folio Alpha 1, is the substance of the next paper in this series.

Discovery

I turn first to the issue of the actual discovery of the manuscripts. For the most part, there seems little debate here, very few points that are still in contention. Yet, it must still be acknowledged that some at least of this apparent agreement by all parties concerned might be – no, I take that back, probably is – due more to successful bureaucratic obfuscation than to the revelation to all involved of the plain unvarnished truth.

It was during the 2004 Olympic Games in Athens that the world first learned of the existence of this priceless collection. I say 'priceless' because I know no other way to express its incredible worth. We have no relative scale of pricelessness. If there were such a scale, say an

Olympic one of from nought to ten, then this would have to score a perfect ten, full marks from all judges.

Here, though, I must first retract somewhat from what I have just said above. It wasn't really that 'the (whole) world' suddenly and gloriously learned of the existence of these precious manuscripts during the Olympics. You and I might have imagined that that would have been a marvellous time for some thundering publicity. But the Greeks didn't see it that way. We strongly believe that there is some very substantial mystery hidden in that decision, but as yet we cannot say what it is.

But first, what in fact was discovered? And how?

Actual discovery – that is, in the true sense of the word, as in first finding – occurred some years before the Olympics, during preparations for the big event, when all of downtown Athens resembled nothing so much as a disparate collection of working quarries, some in good working order and some (most?) not. Many of these quarry-cum-construction holes went down a long way, and many of them revealed other treasures from times long ago, even millennia past. None so great, however, as what we have here.

There were three workmen involved, two young fellows and an old bloke. Just labourers, these three, not skilled craftsmen and all only recently enticed into the city from their home village in the Atlas mountains to help alleviate the desperate shortage of construction manpower needed to put on the Olympic show. Decidedly, they were not literary scholars.

But, probably, they were drunk. It was mid-afternoon; they should have been on their siesta break. And they should not have had all that ouzo at lunchtime. And – and here again so-called 'official' versions of the events are decidedly scraggy around the edges – there is considerable uncertainty as to how, let alone why, they were at the very bottom of one of the deepest construction holes, right on top of the ancient city. It was later determined that this hole had been dug ten metres too deep anyway. But, presciently as it turned out, as close as construction could get to the Parthenon.

Nevertheless, they were indeed discovered at the bottom of said hole, and discovered with them was what in turn they had discovered. Or rather, what they had fortuitously stumbled upon. For the old guy, in the depth of his cups and for reasons known only to himself, had decided that, as far down as they were, they must surely have been close to oil. He decided to dig for it.

After a few wild and rather random slashes with his shovel, he broke through what seemed like the top or roof of a small cavern. It immediately scared him no end, for in his youth he had been a part-time gravedigger and his discovery looked to him all too much like an ancient tomb. And even he well knew that grave robbers could usually look forward to only a short-term future.

Not so his younger companions. They hadn't read all the grave-robber nonsense that seemed to worry their friend. Indeed, they were game, even keen, to explore further, perhaps now, even if not exactly sober, then not completely inebriated either. They took turns on the one shovel between them and proceeded to enlarge the entrance to this underground chamber.

Please pardon me a moment here, but I must repeat that details of all and everything to do with this find, no matter how trivial they might appear to be, have now come under the provisions of a very hastily prepared Antiquities Secrets Act – subsequently, very quickly and highly surreptitiously passed by the Greek parliament. None but the privileged few (which does not include the Pericles committee) are supposed to know or to be told anything. Some details of course are indeed available, if you know about them, and mostly gained by the committee before the Act was passed. You will have to take my word for the rest. Sources too are sacred. No doubt, all will eventually be revealed in due and proper course. Which may be a long time coming.

But back to our hole in the ground. Our three friends there soon saw that indeed it could well have been an ancient burial chamber, an ancient chamber of some sort anyway, but at first glance not very large, overall perhaps two to three metres wide by a little longer, and no more than a metre and a half deep. Despite further serious protestations from the older workman, but eventually accompanied by his fervent religious invocations for protection, one of the younger ones, a short guy of thin and wiry build, jumped down into the hole to explore.

Two things were immediately obvious. First, lined up on – or rather in – both walls, with only a narrow corridor between them, were a series of what, if they had been bigger, he would probably have assumed to be coffins. But these, boxes shall we call them, were much smaller, roughly much the dimensions as a modern but rather large briefcase. There were later found to be seven of these boxes in each wall, very carefully slotted into precisely carved holes, with the holes and containers, though each one was horizontal, arranged in a delicate curve, from top to bottom, along the wall. A right-hand curve on one side, a left-hand curve on the other.

Second, with more of the luck that seemed to be accompanying them that day, they had broken into a section of the roof almost directly above the small chamber's central corridor. Indeed, if they had first hit immediately above either wall and their rows of stacked boxes it is most unlikely that they would have broken through at all. For both walls and containers were constructed of some specially treated marble and as everything was so very neatly slotted into its appropriate place a mere shovel would never have cracked open the ancient chamber.

That was about as far as these three could take their find. By this time, substantial activity had started up again back on the surface, at the edge of the hole. Worse still, however, one of the huge dredging machines used to dig out the hole had swung back into action, primarily to elongate rather than deepen the excavation, and its huge bucket dropped perilously close to the three men at the bottom. Remember, it was not (actually still is not) clear why the men were there in the first place and their workmates up top had no idea that they were there.

Their cries of alarm were eventually heard. Then, but only after much frantic shouting and other noisy carry-on that could be expected in such a situation, dredging stopped and our three soon-to-be-declared heroes were rescued from their hole in the ground. But, as is always the way in such situations, they were at first not believed. Even ridiculed in this particular case, since somebody knew about the ouzo.

Then, however, just as soon as someone more sensible, and more sober, in charge of the crew realised the truth of the story being told, the only truly superb management piece in the entire Olympic organisational machinery associated with the preparation for the games immediately, smoothly and very efficiently leapt into action. Everyone, but everyone, had agreed before any construction in the city had ever started that whenever and wherever they started digging holes the odds were good that they would unearth some ancient treasures of some sort. Clearly this looked like one of those occasions.

The appropriate cultural official was quickly notified. She and her preliminary evaluation team arrived within minutes, and within even fewer minutes, once the potential enormous significance of the find was fully realised, all work on the hole stopped, the police were notified and the area immediately roped off.

All of which is, of course, another very good reason why the rest of the world thought that the Greeks were exceedingly slow in their preparations for the Olympics. Given the magnitude and significance of the find there, work on this particular site necessarily stopped for many months. Indeed, final construction work here was completed only a week before the opening ceremony.

Before I turn to a description of how we (that is, the Pericles committee) came to learn of this remarkable finding, let me cover here all that needs to be said further in this paper – that is, some few words about what was actually found, about both the chamber and its contents.

The chamber and its contents

First, there is not just one but rather seven chambers at that same depth, apparently all essentially identical in size, and possibly contents, and all arranged in a small circle, with the central corridor of each linked to and radiating out from the central core of the circle. Of critical importance, however, although there are only seven chambers, there are eight corridors leading off the central open space. This eighth corridor leads to, and thus links all of the individual chambers with, the very lowest levels of the Parthenon. It appears that all significant openings, however, both to the Parthenon and to each individual chamber, were protected by hermetically sealed doors.

None of this, apart from the initial chamber, has yet been disturbed. Or not that we know of. Highly sophisticated and accurate underground surveying technology has revealed the presence of all of this intricate structure. The only actual contents so far revealed have been those found in the first room.

Second, as I indicated above, this chamber contained precisely and accurately slotted into place along both of its side walls the same number (seven) of identical-sized containers, each apparently made by some superb stonemason or marble master craftsman. The bottom, all sides and the lids of each of these containers are constructed of very thin but very strong marble, hardened in some way by a special process, any details of which have long been lost, and very finely polished. All fitted together to make a seal that was remarkably tight – if left undisturbed!

Once revealed and removed from its place in the stack, however – and the wall adjacent to one such box had partially crumbled from the first shovel entry – any box could have its seal readily broken and its contents revealed simply by sliding the lid very carefully and completely evenly across the sides. All attempts to break the seal in any other manner failed completely. And, moreover, each seal had been so complete that the contents of each box had apparently been perfectly preserved in its original condition for, possibly, two thousand years or more. Keeping them preserved for even a few further years in this highly polluted day and age is another challenge again.

Third, and most importantly, what was in each box? The answer to this question reveals the true magnitude of this accidental discovery by our three, somewhat less than sober, workmen.

The first marble box, the one initially dislodged by accident and apparently the only one so far opened, contained seven seemingly identical manuscripts – that is, each contained seven sections of seven 'pages', each page covered with small but clearly elegant script and all bound together in a manner surprisingly resembling a modern book

At this point, just two characteristics of these remarkable documents will be described, albeit only very briefly: namely the physical nature of these 'books' and some indication of their contents – that is, of the text they bear.

Thus, what do we know so far of the physical attributes of these ancient books? In particular, first, do we have any idea as to how old they might be? It would seem that either accurate carbon or other radioactive dating has not yet been done, or alternatively that the relevant authorities are being exceedingly cautious about releasing the results. This of course is particularly important. Obviously some (many?) would like to claim that the documents so far found are indeed originals, while others, the more conservative scholars, lean to the theory that these are but later copies. But, even if so, then how much later?

Despite this seemingly-far-fetched conclusion, as far as science can tell at the moment, the parchment used for the manuscripts was manufactured not from any previously recognisable ancient paper but from the treated skin of some currently unknown creature, possibly even a pterosaur. And for 'ink' the author may well have used a long-forgotten recipe based on blood, probably animal or bird but possibly human. Some useful work here for the DNA boffins, as well for those handling the carbon and other dating techniques.

The Chronicles

As for the actual text itself, just three important features can appropriately be revealed in this introductory paper: the language used, the possible authorship, and the general nature of the writing. What was in fact written comes later.

One, the language. Perhaps just as one would expect from the location in which the documents were found, the language used appears to be ancient Greek. Not, however, ancient or classical Greek as we generally know it, but some previously unknown variant, proto-Greek perhaps. This is clearly not the language of Homer nor Plato. Very close to the true form, yes, but with sufficient slight and subtle modifications to indicate something like a regional dialect. In the spoken form, it would probably have been recognised as an accent, most likely up-country or from one of the islands. (One of the literary scholars on our committee has called it 'woggerel', as in ethnic doggerel.) Even stranger perhaps, the stories – for that is what they mostly are – are told, or at least written down, in verse format. Each line has seven words, each stanza has seven lines, and each page contains seven stanzas.

Two, while the author or scribe – or authors and scribes – responsible for the writings in the books we have seen to this point was almost certainly not an Athenian, he (I say 'he' for convenience; there is enough internal evidence to indicate that it could equally well have been 'she') was definitely a scholar and an artist. The writing itself is exquisitely executed and the contents – well, judge for yourself from the initial translations that we shall provide in the next papers in this series. My own assessment is that the actual author, I favour only one, was an extremely gifted storyteller and that his stories were written down, as I indicated earlier in exquisite script, by a female companion or colleague. She may well have, probably did, embellish the original stories with some tales of her own.

Three, the stories are placed in a fascinating concept or context of 'time'. All of the events depicted in the texts so far translated, or at least those events for which we have other historical records, are known to have occurred some centuries before the birth of Christ. Yet interwoven with these, sometimes inextricably so, are characters and events known otherwise only in Greek mythology. We assess that the author, the original storyteller, is convinced that time is not a flowing and linear continuum of past, present and future, but rather a circular or better spherical dimension in which we are all caught up and all the events of which are continually present (relevant) to us at all times. There is a similarity here both with Einstein's notion of space being curved, not flat and, more particularly, with the Australian Aborigine's notion of the Dreamtime. *The Chronicles of Pericles* are stories of a Greek dreamtime.

Four, we also know now that the central character in all of these stories, again as so far revealed, appears to be the Greek general and statesman Pericles, and for this reason the whole collection is known as *The Chronicles of Pericles*. Many of his 'relatives' in the stories, especially the more prominent ones, have the same patronymic 'Peri' in their name, such as for instance Pericless (possible a younger brother) and Pericmore (an uncle?). Occasionally the prefix 'Per' appears for some possible relative, but this may indicate an illegitimate or bastard origin.

Our own historical records tell us that a Pericles flourished (really quite a delightful word, especially in this context) in the middle of the fifth century BC, a period of great glory for the city of Athens. But, again from all other internal evidence, it would also seem that the broad sweep of historical time covered by the writer – or, who knows, writers – of these manuscripts and in which Pericles features prominently, embraced much time both well before and well after our historical Pericles. Further examination of the text itself should – well, might – reveal some answers to this conundrum.

Further discovery

Finally I return to the point earlier in this paper where I broke off the story of the 'discovery' of the *Chronicles*. How did anybody other than the relevant Greek authorities, and in particular how did the Pericles committee, come to learn of their existence?

It was at the time of the games themselves. Some few Olympic visitors, who are all now regarding themselves as very lucky individuals, did indeed come to learn something of this whole incredible story. We are now the members of the Pericles committee. And it was all an accident anyway. Really a complete shambles, in fact, for no way did the authorities then, nor even more so now, want as much as a mere whiff of the presence of this treasure to escape their tight control. 'Remember the Elgin Marbles' was their battle cry then. It still is.

As far as we deem it to be relevant, reliable and politic, we can disclose the following account. Several of us – tourists, shall we say, and leave it at that – were in Athens during the first week of the games. But given that there is a limit to the amount that even a true aficionado of synchronised swimming can take, and for us non-fanatics that limit was set fairly low, we deserted the swimming centre for that day and decided to explore some of the more well-recognised cultural attractions of the ancient city. The guidebooks were full of possibilities.

Sadly, at least for others but certainly not for us, those books missed the greatest possibility of them all. After visiting and greatly admiring the Parthenon (obviously an interesting coincidence as it transpired), we turned down a small side street, little more than an alleyway, which we were assured would lead us to the next attraction on our list.

Part way along, on the left-hand side, an apparently very old two- or three-storey building was undergoing some renovation and/ or reconstruction. As part of the usual construction and demolition debris surrounding such an enterprise, there was in the alleyway, and almost blocking it, a very large and very dilapidated rubbish container. And it was full. More than full, though, it was overflowing.

And this was just one of the relevant blunders surrounding the whole hilarious exercise. At least we thought it was hilarious, especially after the event. The Greek government was not amused.

It turned out, as we subsequently discovered, that this particular bin was supposed to have been taken away and emptied that same morning. But, again as we understand it, the truck coming with its replacement had been first delayed, along of course with everyone else on the streets, by city traffic and had then broken down. It hit a pothole, another not-infrequent hazard on the streets of Athens at that time, and had snapped an axle.

It then seemed clear, at least to the crew involved, that they needed, even deserved, a break. Which naturally extended into lunchtime and which, just as naturally, involved the downing of some, possibly copious, quantity of ouzo. It seems that ouzo features quite prominently in this whole story.

But back to our alleyway and the overflowing container. The upshot of the morning's adventure, as we have seen, was that the container had not been replaced. More importantly, however, the workmen inside the building were either oblivious to this or did not care. Either way they continued to tip their debris down the wooden chute temporarily attached to the building for just that purpose and, supposedly, into the bin. Or rather, now, into the alleyway surrounding the bin.

Thus, just as we approached, another wheelbarrow load came tumbling down from the second floor onto the bin and then into the alleyway. Right at our feet, in fact, for several of us had to jump away to avoid being collected by a tumbling jumble of bricks, stone, paper, dust and who knows what else.

But it was the 'what else' that really mattered – and is the whole subject of this discourse. When the dust from the discarded construction debris finally settled somewhat, we were amazed to find, in amidst the rest of the rubbish, something that was clearly not rubbish. At first glance, this seemed to be some form of box or container, about the size and shape of an oversize briefcase. But it was made of marble, a unique and highly polished marble, as we were soon to discover.

Moreover, the lid of this container had slipped off, apparently dislodged when the case hit the bottom at a very precise angle (this angle was critically important, we later discovered) and the contents had in turn been scattered onto the pavement. Both the box and its contents immediately caught our attention. We were fascinated. Perhaps at first more so with the contents. These were clearly manuscripts of some sort, the pages loosely bound at the edges as in a modern book, but clearly of no ordinary paper. One of our number is an amateur, but very gifted, bibliophile who specialises in ancient works. His quick on-the-site initial assessment was that we had stumbled upon something especially important in this field which, given its location, we might well even then consider even to be monumentally important.

We hastily gathered up all of the separate scripts that we could find – there were seven of them – and the marble box as well. This too, both from its material and shape and from the obvious, even there, exquisite workmanship that had gone into its construction further convinced us, if any were needed, that ours was indeed a dramatic discovery.

Before, however, I recount the astounding series of misadventures that led to this precious box and its contents being unceremoniously dumped out of the window of an old and abandoned building undergoing renovation, I shall finish this brief account of the committee's involvement in all of this. That is, by simply saying that what has been described so far is all that will be described. At least here and for the present. Discretion at times being the better part of valour, as they say, I shall merely state that the box and its contents are now safely, securely and undamaged further back where they truly belong, in the hands of the Greek Department of Antiquities. The committee has 'copies' of what it needs.

So what did happen in that old building around the corner from the Parthenon? We expect that ouzo again played a significant role, but we can't be quite certain. We do know, however, that the building was due to become, for a short while at least, an undisclosed and unpublicised repository (remember, secrecy was for some unknown reason all-important) for whatever was removed from that ancient chamber deep in the ground adjacent to the Parthenon.

Only a few of the precious boxes has been removed so far and these had been temporarily stored, under tight control, within the main ministry complex. This present building, when renovated, was to become some form of maximum-security annex. Unfortunately – for the Greek government, that is, but obviously not for us – the several parties involved in the renovations and the subsequent transfer of the precious boxes lost track of each other's progress.

As expected and as usual at that time, the renovations were delayed. Very delayed. But somehow, this simple piece of information had not been passed on to, or had escaped from, those in charge of the document transfer.

Indeed, the first box had been taken over to its intended new home first thing just on the morning that the committee happened by the building. But the box was heavy and the workman involved was, not unreasonably, disinclined to carry it all the way back to the ministry until he had ascertained what was supposed to be going on. So he put it down. But where? Well, amongst the general building confusion on that level there were few well-cleared spaces at any acceptable height above the floor. So he picked the only one obviously available – an apparently disused wheelbarrow off to one side from where the major work seemed to be then concentrated.

Now the unique marble of which the box was constructed, bottom, sides and top, was of a distinctive mottled appearance. This colouring was not unlike military camouflage, which indeed was why it and its companions had seemed to blend in so well into the walls of the chamber where they were originally found. And why this particular box went completely unnoticed when a shovelful or two of broken bricks had been inadvertently dumped on top of it. The wheelbarrow in question was far from disused – all tools were desperately needed if this project were ever to be finished.

But what of the workman who brought it over? It seems that when he went back to the ministry building, his immediate supervisor was off sick. (Well, we were told sick). And all things being as they were at that time – that is, bordering on absolute chaos – it was mid-afternoon before he could find anyone with any authority to tell him what to do next. By which time of course, the fateful wheelbarrow had been filled and its contents subsequently dumped out the window. And, ultimately, into the fortuitously waiting and eagerly welcoming hands of the Pericles committee. Who, quite fittingly, subsequently celebrated with a little (?) ouzo.

Still a Good Idea

Now here's a way to live your day, to keep your life free of strife, should ever you care to try. It won't kill you, may even thrill you, if you would but dare to try.

Not so easy, that's a fact, but what else is there in life to keep your soul intact? It's not at all a duty, just something sweet and fruity, every day to do indeed one simple deed, an unpremeditated act, of kindness or of beauty.

Think of the difference you could make, big or small, give or take, a simple thing indeed. Just find, within your heart and mind, to try each day some kind or beauty deed.

A word, a smile, you needn't go the final mile. Just think about the pleasure, a little treasure in the sun, that you could bring along, right along, with just a little kindness done.

Or if it's elegance that you admire, to things of beauty you aspire, then seek it out with fire. So that amidst the dross that might come your way you could discover, then recover, much that is gold, not loss, within your day.

So don't delay as you go your way, every day, work or play, with just a little tact try an unpremeditated act, of kindness or of beauty. For joy, not duty.

A Different Dialogue on the Road to Emmaus

'Was not our heart burning within us while he was…
explaining to us the Scriptures' Luke, 24, 32

They were odd companions to be on the road together. Not exactly a hare-and-tortoise type combination, though Scientus had indeed overtaken Scriptus, but rather an unusual – though ultimately seen to be highly complementary – pairing of personalities and outlooks, of experiences and talents.

Scientus, as you might expect, while not exactly skinny was nevertheless lean and angular, fit and always eager to move on. Some might have said he had 'a lean and hungry look'; true, but in this particular case not also 'dangerous'. He was indeed hungry for knowledge, and understanding too, keen always to move on to the next stage in his quest, to turn the next corner or breast the next rise and thus to see and to examine the newer vista, the next challenge of the unknown.

It would not be hard to imagine him in a white coat, probably a little worn and stained, with pens and pencils in his pocket and, of course, talking. Always talking. You might have wanted him to stop occasionally, to take a deep breath and listen for a change. But perhaps only a minor blemish. He certainly seemed to know what he was talking about.

While Scriptus, by contrast – ah yes, by contrast – though not really short and dumpy, might at first glance have appeared that way. He was certainly solid; indeed, he had quite an air of solidarity, dependability, about him. This seemed to match his tone of voice, his general demeanour, a rather quiet air of authority. Older, too. Did I mention that Scientus was younger – or at least that he seemed to be?

No white coat could be imagined for this one, though; more likely a tweed jacket perhaps. And surely a pipe, if maybe only now and then. Scientus, true to his profession, had given up tobacco long ago. Though it was harder to give up entirely the occasional craving.

Scriptus, as you might expect, was – or perhaps just appeared to be – slower and steadier in thought and action. He was in less of a hurry, keener to explore the nooks and crannies of the current landscape, to plumb it for its depths of meaning before moving on beyond the next bend or over the next hill. You could say perhaps that it was understanding first that he was seeking, then the knowledge would follow. And of course he listened much more than he spoke.

But along the road they were clearly both following, Scientus and Scriptus fell naturally into a genial companionship. For what seemed likely to be rewarded with good fellowship Scientus was prepared to slow down a little, while Scriptus could easily more along a little faster than was his usual want. They got to talking.

'Before you caught up with me,' said Scriptus softly, 'I had been thinking about beginnings. How did all of this –' he waved his arm about rather vaguely, as though to encompass not only the land and sky around and the gentle river, the bank of which their road was following, but also Scientus and himself '– how did all this come about? There must surely have been a beginning, sometime, someplace, yet all is continually changing. This river is flowing past us, we are getting older, but hopefully not too much so before we reach our destination, these flies that are annoying us will soon be dead and gone. Though, unfortunately, soon replaced by others. Was there a start to all this change? How did it start, I wonder? And will it end – or will it continue forever? The ancient books have much to say about these mysteries and I confess that I have been reading them again a lot lately.'

At this point he stopped abruptly and turned to face Scientus. 'Though I must say that, right now, I am rather more concerned about the beginning than the end.' He laughed then, as the gentle irony of that position suddenly struck him. 'Perhaps, though, I should be more

worried about the end – I reckon that for you and me that is going to
be a much more personal business than I can remember any beginning
having been.'

'Funny that you should ask,' replied Scientus, in a tone not exactly
sharp but rather assured, confident, as if he could quite easily supply
the answers, or at least pretty good answers, to Scriptus's age-old
question. And to any other similar problems he might have.

'Now this just happens to be my major line of study, my area of
expertise – if I may be so bold as to claim expert status in the field.'
Scientus, unlike many of his fellow practitioners, was genuinely
humble about the degree to which he, or any other, could assert that
absolute truth was to be found, at least ultimately if not indeed not
currently, within their discipline alone.

'Books and other writings, yes, they are a great place to start. Who
was it said in this regard, "If I have been able to see further, it has been
because I could stand on the shoulders of giants"?'

'Newton,' murmured Scriptus quietly, not wanting to appear more
knowledgeable in science than his companion should have been.

'Yes, of course,' continued Scientus, not in the least annoyed nor
embarrassed, 'but in this particular field I'm really thinking rather of
those others who contributed more directly to the specific science
involved. There were some real characters among them, let me tell you.'

A keen observer might have noticed a subtle change in Scientus's
mien and manner here. In Scriptus's presence, his tone softened a
little, he relaxed a little, so that while still authoritative and assertive
he could nevertheless continue more in a conversational rather than
a lecturing mode. Science, he seemed to be realising, could be just as
believable, perhaps even more so, if explained in common rather than
just scientific terminology.

'Where we stand today on this question of beginnings, particularly
the biological perspective on it, what you might call current modern
understanding – and we can talk more about this later if you wish
– was really first brought together, the whole action kick-started, if

you like, by young Charlie Darwin and his musings during his trip to the South Pacific on the good ship *Beagle*. Amazing, isn't it? That was written nearly a hundred and fifty years ago and we still reckon that he got it mostly right.'

'Mmm,' was about all that Scriptus could add just then, though he was of course wondering if what had been first written down some 2,500 years ago could also be still 'mostly right'.

This conversation was developing well.

So Scientus continued, unaware of or just unconcerned by any apparent interruption. 'Then we had that very clever priest fellow Greg Mendel, some sort of monk or hermit, I think he was, Romania, was it, or Bulgaria, I can never remember which.'

'Moravia,' suggested Scriptus, again rather quietly, 'or a part of Austria as it was then.'

'Yes, Austria, of course, but then you would know more that sort of stuff than I would. But monk or not, that Mendel really thought things through. Of course there has been some concern that maybe his gardener – he worked with peas, you know – might have been a tad over-zealous in getting the precise numbers that his boss wanted, but that aside it was the good father's concepts that were important. Must have been that contemplative life he led – all that deep thinking must have helped.'

'True,' murmured Scriptus, 'a little thinking can surely go a long way. And what I have been thinking,' he then continued in his own rather contemplative way, almost as if just thinking aloud, 'is that really whoever tries to sell us a story about the origin of this universe of ours and everything in it, particularly physical as well as biological origins, be it your Stephen Hawking,' Scriptus wasn't as dumb about modern science as he might have been seen to appear, 'or those ancient Jewish priests I've been reading again, or indeed anyone in between, really has to address just two very simple questions – simple on the surface, that is, but realistically very profound. And of course we have first to get the questions right before we can possibly hope to get the answers right.'

To which his companion nodded vigorous assent.

'Thus first, we might wonder what happened, what actually occurred, do you think? Only then second, I believe, can we ask how or why did it happen, what made it happen? Perhaps only the first of these is a true scientific question, while the second might appeal more just to those with a theological bent.'

'Perhaps so, perhaps not,' conceded Scientus, 'your notion of two separate questions is an important one to hold on to, but my scientific colleagues and I would like to think that we could address the second question just as well as the first. Causes as well as effects are our province too.'

'But tell me, good friend, what do your ancient authors have to say about all this? The Book of Genesis, I assume, is mostly what you have in mind. I know it, or rather I should say I know of it, but what is the modern take?'

'Yes, true,' continued Scriptus, more or less still just thinking aloud, 'Genesis, or at least what we now describe as its first two chapters' (actually Genesis 1:1–27; 2:7 and 21–23 mainly, if you care to look it up) 'seem to have most to say about what you might call the consensus, or at least the Hebrew consensus, of the many creation ideas around at the time it was written.'

'Creation myths, I reckon, most people seem to call them now,' was a swift interjection from Scientus.

'Quite so,' agreed Scriptus cheerfully, 'but first, let me tell you a little about how it all came to be written down, for that is quite important too, before I seek your comments on what was in fact written.'

At this, Scriptus had to smile a little at himself, for he could see that if he were not careful, he could so easily slip into the lecturing mode more often associated with the scientist than the scripture scholar.

'Today we reckon that the first written versions of Genesis I appeared around the beginning of the 6th century BC. Or BCE, as you probably more often refer to it. At that time a rather rag-tag mob of Hebrews had struggled back to their beloved Jerusalem, which they had long considered, even during prolonged absences, to be their true physical and spiritual home. They had recently escaped from captivity in Babylon – or perhaps had been kicked out, the history there is a little vague – and had made their way back to their historic homeland. And what a mess they found. Jerusalem, or what was left of it, virtually in ruins, the sacred Temple of Solomon, their most precious place of worship, destroyed. Now at this point – that, is upon their arrival back home and their surveying of the damage done – the priestly class amongst the Hebrews took over. Of course priests seem always to be doing this, I must admit,' he added rather quickly, before his companion could make the same observation, which indeed he had appeared about to do.

'Thus the priests were particularly concerned that their flock, in these otherwise disheartening circumstances, should still maintain – indeed, even strengthen – their traditional faith both in their one true God (Yahweh, as they tended to call him at that time) and in their own privileged position as His "Chosen People". So they – the priests, that is – reckoned particularly that now that their primary physical place of worship (the Temple) was unavailable – at least until they could repair it, and that would take a good long time – then it would be critically helpful if the people could have available a series of relevant texts, if what was needed to be known, and remembered, and believed, could indeed be written down. They had just come from Babylon, don't forget, where writing was already a big thing. Until that time most of their beliefs had all been just an oral history. Just hearsay, some might say.'

Scientus just smiled at all of this. He chose not to interrupt, as his scientific training and personal inclination might have prompted him to do. It was a pleasantly clear and sunny day and with little else to do while travelling than listening to ancient myths and fairy tales, well told by an amiable companion with a good choice of words, was as pleasant a way as any to spend his time.

'So those ancient Hebrew priests were the first to give us the creation story, or perhaps more correctly the first written version of it, as they understood it at the time. Now, remember those two initial questions we agreed about – essentially the what and the how. Well, since their primary task was to talk up God, those priestly scribes tackled the second question first. And their answer? Simple. God did it! God was responsible for the whole box and dice. "In the beginning God created the heavens and the earth." They didn't set out to"prove" that God was responsible – for them, and for all those who followed them, that was a given. Only then did they give their take on the what problem. What actually happened way back then.'

Scientus just had to interrupt here. He felt he had been far too quiet for far too long. 'But, my friend,' he asked, just a trifle craftily, 'if they had in fact wanted to prove that God did it all, even that God simply existed, do you think that they could have done it? Could you? Today?'

'Ho, ho,' laughed Scriptus, delighted at last to be challenged. 'As my children would say, no problem! No problem at all.'

'What,' the scientist in Scientus, the sceptic in him, swiftly interjected. 'You must surely be joking. We all know that such "proof" just isn't possible.'

'Not quite,' countered Scriptus, in no way concerned at the apparent vehemence in Scientus's tone, 'and no, I am not joking at all. As I said, to construct a proof of the existence of God is no problem at all. The real problem, the key question, is not "Can you prove it?" but rather "Will you believe the proof when I do?" Obviously I do believe it, but you and your scientific colleagues, as scientists, do not. And I cannot fault you for that, for indeed there is no scientific proof. None at all. I understand and appreciate that, but I do ask you to consider whether or not there might be acceptable proof other than scientific proof.'

This caused them both to stop and wonder, caused a long gap in an otherwise almost unbroken conversation.

Not wishing to extend a rift between them, Scriptus was the first to pick up again the threads of their conversation, from just before that point about proof – where they had essentially agreed to disagree. 'Can we come back to all that later, for do let me finish the Genesis creation story. There is much there about which I would value your comments. As a scientist. Those scribes I talked of, once they had disposed to their satisfaction of the question of how it all happened, and obviously disposed of it in God's favour in just that one, all-encompassing opening sentence, for that was the whole purpose of the exercise, then turned their attention to the first question we asked earlier. That is, what did in actual fact happen? If God did it, then just what did He actually do? Just what sequence of events did He set in motion? And this, my good friend Scientus, is exactly where you come in. Can you perhaps tell me just how well, or not, do the rest of the relevant parts of Genesis fit with what current science seems to be telling us about its take on the same sequence of events? Remarkably well, it seems to me, but then that is just me. You are the scientist.'

'Delighted,' agreed Scientus cheerfully. 'I'll be happy to straighten you out.'

Now being 'straightened out' was clearly not quite what Scriptus had in mind, but he let it pass. He was eager to continue his story. And to rebuild their earlier amicable companionship. 'First up, of course, our early priests, as does indeed anybody else who tackles this theme, had one great big problem getting started. How (I almost said "how on earth") do you describe what was "present" – if that is the appropriate word, or perhaps just what "was" – before it all happened? How do you describe absolute nothing? To me, with just a little poetic licence, "the earth was waste and void; darkness covered the abyss" seems to do a pretty good job.'

'Not bad,' agreed Scientus, 'not bad at all. I don't think that science has yet gotten round to describing the state of affairs just before the Big Bang. Or perhaps hasn't yet found the right words to describe it. The Big Bang,' he added quickly, 'you are of course familiar with that theory?' He wasn't sure how much science his companion knew.

'Well, yes,' replied Scriptus, though somewhat hesitatingly, 'or perhaps, more like you and the Book of Genesis, I know of the theory more by name rather than by any of the detail. I believe I did once see it described as the sudden massive explosion of an infinitesimally small and infinitely dense core of matter, but even that much leaves me gasping.'

'Well, that's perhaps not too bad a description,' conceded Scientus, but just as he was about to launch into a further long technical explanation Scriptus forestalled him.

'Before we get too engrossed with the technicalities of the Big Bang theory, however, and how the ancients might have foreseen the concept, there is one other aspect of the very beginning that I should like to hear you comment upon. Though it isn't really a part of the science involved, it might nevertheless intrigue you. Those priestly scholars way back then had another practical dilemma getting started on their creation story. Obviously – obvious for them, that is – there couldn't have been completely the "absolute nothing" I referred to earlier, for clearly if God were to be involved, then He had to be out there, somewhere, waiting to work His magic. They agreed that there was an absence of anything and everything that we on earth know anything at all about, but if God were around at the time then logically He had to be somewhere. How does "and the spirit of God was stirring above the waters" sound to you? Though before you answer that,' he continued quickly, 'I should mention that the descriptor, "the waters", gets a lot of good press in Genesis. Those ancient Hebrews (or whoever they were) who carried this story along through time well before our priest friends got round to writing it all down clearly found a great deal of meaning and symbolism in water. In some ways, perhaps, synonymous with life itself. Certainly there is no life without it. Was there any life before it? And thus in this specific context, this verse from Genesis, as elsewhere in the scriptures, "the waters" seems frequently to be synonymous with the notion of "chaos" – a lack of order, arising specifically from a lack of anything at all to order.'

Maybe neither Scientus nor Scriptus was thinking much about it at the time, but we all really do need, for all sorts of pressing reasons, for modern science to tell us more of the specific origin of the water molecule – a substance with a very large and continually increasing list of 'unique' and fascinating characteristics. This may be even more important, from an evolutionary perspective, than our knowing about the origins of more complex molecules such as amino acids and DNA.

'Well,' replied Scientus, rather more slowly this time, for he really hadn't thought much about all this before, 'as you would know, I don't go much for the God bit, but I do agree that "the waters" concept does call for some interesting speculation. Or better, some interesting research. And I do concede that while science is making great strides in determining what happened just after the Big Bang, even in the first few milliseconds following it, I think science is still having some considerable difficulty coming to grips with the milliseconds just before the Big Bang.'

'OK then,' continued Scriptus cheerfully, as he took up once more the Genesis story, 'so far so good for what was around and happening – clearly nothing at all – before it all happened. What next? If, as I think I detect that you agree, the modern scientific version of whatever it was that got the whole works rolling, set the whole show on the road, as it were, is some variant of the Big Bang hypothesis – that "infinitesimally" small and "infinitely" dense core of matter suddenly exploding – then what does Genesis say about all that? Actually, right there and then, God's very first creative act, "Let there be light." And bingo! There was light! Day one, the good book describes it. This still seems to me to be about as accurate or meaningful a description as one could get without delving too deeply into both the general theory of relativity and quantum mechanics. Those courses were probably not available, even to any priests, at the time anyway.'

To which Scientus added, 'Why, yes. And again forgoing any God connection for the moment, I can readily agree that no matter what else happened I too could be confident that to any casual observer around at the time then, light would definitely have been the first thing noticed.'

(I must interpose here that although I can't speak for Scriptus, nevertheless personally I much prefer the Latin version of that phrase in Genesis, *fiat lux*, as God's first recorded words, as sounding much more dramatic. But I'm not sure that God would have needed any language at all to express his thoughts. I wonder how it sounds in Aramaic, if that were the language first used in the written version.)

'But hang on a tick,' Scientus continued, mainly in order to grasp back the conversational initiative, 'you mentioned something there about "day one"'. Don't you think that before we proceed further we need to clarify here just what those early writers might have meant by their use of the specific term "day" in all of this? I don't follow all the arguments, obviously, no point really, but don't those ratbag Creationists keep banging on about how Genesis proves that their God did all his magic tricks, including creating man, in one specific week back in March, 4004 BCE? Or somewhere around then.'

'Good point,' agreed his companion, 'and I too believe that the Creationist mob is completely off beam. Genesis makes no attempt to "prove" anything, certainly not to prove anything scientifically. We can safely leave scientific proof to the scientists. Though of course we scriptural scholars are nevertheless keen to hear what facts science can provide to help us further understand the significance of the Genesis story. That's why I am particularly enjoying our conversation today. But how I do digress. While any notion of a twenty-four-hour type day seems not to have arisen until much later in the process — "day" four perhaps – nevertheless here, right at the beginning, we do have, "God separated the light from the darkness, calling the light Day and the darkness Night".'

'Indeed,' countered Scientus, 'as I said, that does calls for some explanation. Is there one?'

'Not sure, really,' admitted Scriptus, 'but at least I do have a theory. But first there is something else I have to tell you, something else those pesky priests appeared to be up to at that time. Another part of their agenda, you might say. You will remember that their primary task at that difficult time, as they saw it, was to keep their, probably unruly, flock in line. Thus, not only did they want to give them a good fix on God, his overwhelming power, majesty and so on, but also they desperately needed to encourage them in their worship of that same God. Now while they themselves could easily worship away all day every day – or at least appear to do so, a strategy not unknown in their modern-day counterparts – the general population could not be so readily similarly occupied. Even then the work of society had to be done, families had to sheltered, clothed and feed and so on. So if they couldn't expect more or less full-time worship, then at least one day in the week could be devoted exclusively to it. Hence the real importance to the priests of the Sabbath, the seventh day in the week. And what better way to instil in their flock a lasting appreciation for the special significance, the sacred nature even, of the Sabbath than to have God himself observing it?

'Now, while the ancient creation story that they were presently writing down was, or at least it seems to me it was, more concerned with getting the sequence of events right rather than with the precise divisions of the time over which it all happened, the priests used this (God-given?) opportunity to fit it all neatly into one working week. Their Babylonian sojourn had probably instilled into them the much earlier concept of a week of seven days. Thus, as I read the story now, while later on the various writers are clearly talking in terms of a "day" as we know it – ending up, as I said, with a Sabbath day of rest at the end of the week – at this point I propose that they are more interested in saying that what God here and subsequently did He did in the light, not in the dark.

'I recognise, however, that our Genesis author does repeatedly use the phrase "and there was evening and morning, the first (or second, third and so on) day", but I take this more to be just clarifying matters for their readers. God did it all in the light, in "daytime", though not under any specific constraint of time as we currently measure it. Coincidentally, though, you might say that it did reinforce the notion that it all happened after light was on the scene. After the Big Bang, if you like.'

Scientus was a little uneasy. He was having something of a problem here. While he couldn't really disagree with anything Scriptus had said so far, he was conscious that he wasn't contributing much to the debate. Surely he had somewhat of an obligation to keep science's end up in this conversation?

Scriptus seemed to have paused, was gathering his thoughts as it were, so Scientus continued the dialogue.

'What then,' he pondered aloud, 'no, wait a sec, I just thought of something that could be relevant here. That word "day", as in separating night from day, do you know if it was exactly the same word – that is, in Aramaic or whatever – as was used for the first, second, third and so on day?'

'Not absolutely sure,' was about the best that Scriptus could do, 'but I think so. Interesting idea, though. I must look into it.'

While Scriptus's words, and perhaps his mind too, trailed off on that thought, Scientus took firm grasp again of the conversation. 'What then,' he asked, picking up from where he had just left off, 'does Genesis then have to say about the next sequence of events? Science seems to be telling us that after that first explosion, that "blinding flash of light", as it were, we then had in place instantly both light and also an immense amount of energy. Though perhaps I could wonder just what we would mean by "in place". Space perhaps?'

'Well,' conceded Scriptus, 'you will have to tell me what it means – scientifically, that is, and if it means anything at all – but how does this sound? Let there be a firmament…dividing the waters that were below the firmament from those that were above it. God called the firmament Heaven. Day two.

'Hang on. Let me think about this a moment.'

Scriptus left him to collect his thoughts.

After a few moments' further consideration of that particular Genesis text, Scientus continued. 'Now while I don't know how you scriptural guys construe it, nevertheless there does seem to me, at first glance anyway, that there could be two rather interesting points in that particular text. First, we again have here – or better, I should say *you* have here – another mention of the waters. And while again agreeing that we (er, you, me, whoever) certainly do need much more work on the significance of this phrase to the Hebrews of the time, I could see that it is not unreasonable to conjecture that "dividing the waters" could be synonymous in this context with "bringing order out of chaos". Although,' he suddenly had another thought, 'perhaps it wouldn't be stretching the imagination too much, nor even stretching poetic licence beyond its elastic limits, that this separating out, even the dividing the light and dark bit before it as well, could be a way of referring to the period after the Big Bang when the whole universe was cooling down, coalescing as it were into its various entities. I could also imagine that the use here of the word "heaven",' Scientus proceeded, as he picked up his previous line of thought, 'is taken to mean in this context not the place where any god or gods might live but rather "the heavens" – that is, everything above and beyond the earth. The use of "space" rather then "the heavens" as synonymous with the sky above is a pretty recent phenomenon. Well, certainly more recent than Genesis.'

It was then Scriptus's turn to take up the running. 'After all that energy (light) and space bit, Genesis now comes not just to the origin of the universe generally, but more specifically to the origin of life. Or, more specifically still, to the origin of life on earth. But first we had to have an earth. "Let the waters below the heavens be gathered into one place and let the dry land appear." (Day three.)'

'Science can't complain about that bit,' conceded Scientus. 'Just more order out of chaos, I reckon. What comes next?'

Scriptus paused a while here before continuing. He had begun to feel a little apprehensive, for he was coming, or rather Genesis was coming, to some really critical stuff. Crunch time for their dialogue, you might say.

'What follows then, and perhaps let me just paraphrase it for you for the moment,' Scriptus eventually offered, 'is the Genesis I version of what seems, at least to me, to be the whole evolutionary sequence just exactly as science – or I think just as science – currently conceives it. "Let the earth bring forth vegetation." (Day three.) "Let the waters abound with life." (Day five.) "Above the earth let winged creatures fly below the firmament of the heavens." (Day five.) "Let the earth bring forth all kinds of living creatures." (Day six.) Then, right at the very end of the line, "Let us make mankind… [M]ale and female He created them." (More work for day six.)'

'Wow,' replied Scientus with considerable surprise. 'Obviously I had never thought about it before, but that indeed is more or less exactly the sequence as modern science believes it to be – vegetation, fish, birds, animals, man. Spot on!'

Scriptus smiled at that, but then continued a little more tentatively, 'You might have noticed, however, that there was a subtle change of wording there at the end. Up until mankind got a guernsey, most of God's creative words were in the manner of "let there be". For mankind, however, God is portrayed as saying "let us make". In this way, the Hebrew priests would appear to be reaffirming their belief, and thus also instilling this belief into their flock, that somehow in this whole sequence mankind is something special. Indeed, the story has not just "let us make mankind" but rather "Let us make mankind in our image. In the image of God he created him. Male and female he created them."'

'Wait up,' Scriptus injected somewhat abruptly at this point, 'I must say science would be less than happy with that bit about "in the image of god". And isn't there something there, later on perhaps, about the first woman rather than just the first man? God supposedly taking a rib from Adam, or some such carry on?'

Before Scriptus could recover from this somewhat unexpected verbal onslaught, Scientus held up his hand. Scientist and lecturer, remember.

'Hold on, though, before you jump in to defend the Bible on that score, let me add that there is something else in the Genesis account you have given so far that does also intrigue me. Perhaps you hadn't thought of it. Don't forget that I am still not conceding your notion of a god behind all this, but as a firm believer in evolutionary theory it does seem rather interesting to me that those ancient scribes, while certainly vigorously insisting upon the creative power of their God – their job, I suppose – nevertheless, as you yourself pointed out a moment ago, they had him saying so often "let" this or that happen. That sounds just as if they reckoned that the whole and complete universe, or should I say rather the potential for the complete universe, had been there right from the beginning and slowly, even every new day if you like, we see that universe slowly but progressively developing, unfolding as it were. The whole concept of evolution in a nutshell, of course, both physical and biological evolution.'

Now that made Scriptus sit up and take notice. He hadn't thought of it that way before, but it did make eminent sense. And that, of course, was why he was delighting in this whole conversation, science throwing a modern light on an ancient text.

Neither he nor any of his scriptural colleagues had ever pretended that the scriptures were in any sense whatsoever 'scientific'. Such ancient writings, merely the written record of even more ancient verbal stories, could hardly be expected to add anything to modern experimental science. Nevertheless, it is indeed intriguing to recognise the extent to which those tales from centuries, even millennia, ago are in so close agreement with what science is telling us today.

While Scriptus was still pondering this mystery, Scientus broke into his thoughts. 'But before you tell me more about the Genesis male and female creation bit, there was yet something else of interest, concern perhaps, in what you have covered already. Am I mistaken or did you not leave out a day there somewhere?'

He was not a scientist for nothing, you know.

'Yes, indeed I did,' conceded his companion, 'for that is one of a number of specific points where I could use your help. As you so cleverly noticed, in the sequence of events our reading of Genesis so far has already covered I did skip the fourth day – the sun, the moon, the stars, all that bit. So let me backtrack a little. "Let there be lights in the firmament of the heavens to separate day from night; let them serve as signs and for the fixing of seasons, days and years... God made the two great lights, the greater light to rule the day and the smaller one to rule the night, and he made the stars." (Day four.)'

Scientus thought about that. 'Mmm, I can see your problem. At least at first glance it would seem clear, as science would certainly hold, that the events of your fourth day would certainly have come before those of the third day. We needed the sun lighting up the earth before we could have any plant life there. How do you see your way out of this dilemma?' he added after a brief pause.

'Actually, I don't,' Scriptus admitted a little ruefully, 'but nevertheless I do have some thoughts about it. As you might have guessed. It seems to me,' he continued, looking down at the path they were following as though some clues might lie hidden there beneath their feet, 'that there are at least two possible theories or options for interpretation here. The first, and perhaps the most obvious suggestion, would simply be that the priestly tradition dealing with that point was wrong – that is, it might have gotten the sequence wrong. Or maybe it was just written down incorrectly. No reason, of course, why that bit – or any of it, for that matter – had to be right, just that all the rest seems to be.

'But also perhaps we could look at it another way. For instance, could we postulate that our sun, our moon and the stars really have little relevance to us until they can be seen from the perspective of the earth? So day three would then indeed come before day four. Or put that another way. Could we suppose that here, as also in some places elsewhere, those priests might have been retelling the traditional tale more in the sequence in which man came to recognise some of these things, not strictly in the order in which they first happened? Thus almost certainly early man would have recognised the very great importance of the plant world – that is, both in his own life and in God's greater scheme of things (the main priestly concern) – before he might have realised the key dependence of plants upon sunlight.'

'Yes,' Scientus started to reply, then paused a little to think about it some more. He then continued, still in the thinker's mode. 'Of course there may well be other explanations for this apparent, or at least possible, inaccuracy in the early story, the "priestly tradition" did you call it then, of the strict sequence of the events of creation. Though, also interestingly, in that verse the scribes certainly seem to have been using the term "day" in its twenty-four-hour sense, at least part of the time. But, back to your main point, if I am discerning correctly your real interest in what I might be able to contribute, then perhaps here is a spot where scientific "truth" might indeed be able to shed some interesting light upon biblical scholarship. Everything else Genesis and you have covered so far has been so scientifically accurate, leaving God out of the equation of course – that is, does seem not unreasonable that science could help out here also.'

To which Scriptus added, but only to himself, 'Or might Genesis, perhaps, have something to say that could help science out a little.' He could think this, of course, but wouldn't dare say it out loud.

Talking and walking can both be tiring. And our companions on the road had been doing a lot of both this day. Nevertheless, their day was still young and the next town was not yet in sight. Moreover, to both of them, their conversation so far had been invigorating. And thus so easy to continue.

After some minutes, in which each was thinking his own thoughts about all that had been said, Scriptus took up the conversation again, picking up from a point where they had left off earlier.

'Would you care to go over with me again an aspect of evolution that we only touched on only so briefly earlier, namely the male/female slant that Genesis takes on the origins of mankind.'

'Gladly,' responded Scientus. 'That whole part of what little I know of the scripture story has always bothered me.'

'Unfortunately, though,' Scriptus interspersed here, 'I am afraid that first I shall have to bore you a little with some more of Scripture Studies 101 that is relative to what we currently believe is how this early part of what we now call Genesis came to be written down. It now seems clear to the various experts in this field that those priest/scribes who first put the stories to paper – or more likely onto some form of treated goatskin – were drawing on two quite separate sources. Still both entirely or predominantly oral sources, but each with a very different provenance.'

As Scriptus gathered his thoughts as to how to present this in as simple a way as possible, Scientus chipped in. 'Interesting. And of course as a scientist I have to agree that one must get one's references right. Credit where credit is due and all that.'

'Just so,' agreed Scriptus. 'You may remember that all of that more or less technical creation stuff that we have already discussed I have already referred to as coming from what is called the Priestly Tradition. And that, mostly chapter 1 in modern texts, was indeed probably first written down around 600 BCE, when the Hebrews returned from Babylon. But the next large section of Genesis, up to and including chapter 11, seems to have come from a much earlier source. This is most often referred to as the Yahwist text, since that is where the Hebrews first referred to their God as Yahweh. And that may have been first written down, at least in part, as early as around 1000 BCE. And for the priests who husbanded all this together, after Babylon, there was yet another compelling reason for doing so. They needed not only to strengthen their flock's faith in their one, true God and in their allegiance to Him, they also needed to strengthen the Hebrews' faith in themselves. Much of Genesis 2–11 has this very much in mind. These were their fundamental traditions. These were their origins as a distinct people, a people favoured by God, these were the important people and the critical events in their history. All good national identity building stuff. Straighten up, stiff upper lip, you know, soldier on, we can prevail against all odds. That's the stuff to give the troops.'

'Ha,' chuckled Scientus, 'I seem to have heard a great deal of this same guff from our own secular priests, the politicians today of all faiths, er, parties. What does it mean to be an Australian, must teach more Australian history, there's more to Australia than Ned Kelly and Waltzing Matilda, you must have heard it too.'

'Too true, too true,' agreed his companion, 'and I probably detect as little sincerity in it all today as you do, important though the debate itself undoubtedly is.'

'But let's get back to some more solid stuff.'

'Earlier, in the Priestly Tradition, God was depicted predominately as the all powerful creator. No mucking around, get on with the job, in time and under budget, that sort of impersonal, no-nonsense sort of attitude. So we have, as you may remember, "let us make mankind… male and female He created them." But now, in subsequent chapters, the Yahwist God is depicted much differently, much more personally. Why, the more romantic of the relevant scholars even see him portrayed there in turn as gardener, sculptor and surgeon – the Garden of Eden, forming all the animals, including man, from the earth, the bit about taking a rib from Adam, remember? But how I do get ahead of myself. And a bit carried away, I must admit. So let me return to where there might be some more science and some less theology for us to discuss. Let us look at "Then the Lord God formed man out of the dust of the ground and breathed into his nostrils the breath of life" (Genesis 2:7).

'Before you comment, however,' Scriptus went on quickly, indeed before Scientus could comment, 'let me suggest to you that, given that the authors at the time did not have a friendly neighbourhood DNA laboratory nearby with which to check out their findings, that again we must remember that said authors were on a commission for some PR work for God, and that some allowance could be made for a little poetic licence, then I would reckon that as a scientist you might find that ancient Genesis II verse as good a single-line summary of the modern theory of evolution of man as could be constructed. It is certainly as good as I have ever seen.'

'Well, yes and no,' conceded Scientus, ever the sceptic, 'but on hearing it now it seems to me that that particular verse should be read in two parts, just one part science, if you like, and the other more theology. I readily agree that "formed man out of the dust of the ground" is perfectly acceptable evolutionary science. Quite beautifully put, really. On the other hand, though, am I not correct in thinking that the second phrase "and breathed into his nostrils the breath of life" is considered by your people as to account for the derivation of the human soul, rather than as anything to do with man's body. And very definitely that is much more a religious than a scientific proposition.'

'*Concedo, concedo*, very true,' Scriptus was quick to reply, 'and of course it goes well with that earlier bit, God's making mankind "in his image". And that too is pure theology, not science at all.'

(An earlier English version of this verse had God forming man "out of the slime of the earth" rather than "out of the dust of the ground". Personally I rather prefer the ring of that, and it may even be a tad more accurate scientifically, but the science is still perfectly clear. Apparently this is how we were formed, ultimately from the earth, and here of course, true to their theme, the Genesis writers have God doing it. Over what time frame they don't say, apart from that ubiquitous 'day'. But on day 6, note, clearly at the end of the evolutionary line. But back to our main story.)

'You know,' Scriptus continued, though somewhat hesitantly, for he did not wish to offend his new-found friend, 'given how close how much of the rest of the story, the theological version if you like, is in agreement with today's strict science, then I must confess that I have a sneaking suspicion that one day science and theology will find themselves in much closer agreement about the notion of a human soul than they are today. Or at least in much less disagreement.'

Scientus could do little more than raise his eyebrows at this. That was really pretty radical stuff and he would have to consider it all much further before he would dare to comment upon such a proposition.

Scriptus did not mind his friend's silence on this point, probably expected it. So he moved on. 'But look,' and he raised his eyes towards the horizon, 'I think we are coming up to our destination. Or at least to mine. Could we leave that last point, until another meeting perhaps, for there is still one more aspect of the creation story that we touched on earlier and one about which I should indeed be grateful for your comments. I refer of course to the male/female bit.'

'Of course,' Scientus replied, 'I'd be happy to look at that – it never did make much sense to me anyway. And I think we have time. What was it again that the ancients had to say about it all?'

'Well,' said Scriptus, 'realistically not very much at all. And that of course is part of the problem. Genesis on this, as on so many topics, is very brief, cryptic almost. Initially we certainly have it clearly and unequivocally laid out in chapter I, the straightforward bit, "male and female he created them". But then in chapter II, the romantic section if you like, we are given some more details given about this particular job lot. "The Lord God cast the man into a deep sleep and, while he slept, took one of his ribs and closed up its place with flesh. And the rib which the Lord God took from the man he made into a woman." Clearly this needs some further explanation. Cries out for it. Any thoughts?'

'Not a clue. Not the faintest idea.' Scientus was brutally honest. 'But surely you must have given it some thought.'

'Why yes, of course,' Scriptus was quick to assert, couldn't have his credentials challenged, 'a great deal of thought. But that doesn't necessarily mean that I have come up with any decent answers.'

'One could say that given the "romantic" tone of that whole part of Genesis, then clearly as the ribs are close anatomically to the heart – and a beating heart is just as clearly the most significant sign that one is living – then for all time woman should be close to man's heart. And just as the ribs protect the heart, then so too mutual protection between man and woman might be assured. More practically, though, I suppose too that a man could spare a rib without too much damage being done. Yet none of all that seems to me to be even close to a genuinely satisfactory explanation. Why, even priests at that time must surely have known that a man does not have one less rib than does a woman.'

'Precisely my point all along,' was Scientus's rather obvious response. 'I am afraid that, at least for now, you can't look to me – nor to science generally, for that matter – for much enlightenment. One idea, though, does occur to me, and I offer it for what it's worth. Do you think that currently you have enough understanding of what might have been the significance of ribs to the ancient Hebrews? Given that you seem to think that everything else is so close to scientific truth, and I concede that you have made this point very well, then maybe there is something more to this fixation on ribs than initially meets the eye.'

'Well, yes,' replied his friend, 'and perhaps I should have mentioned this first. In Sumerian, at least, another language with which those very early writers were probably familiar, the word for "rib" is the same as that for "life". Eve's taking of a rib from Adam was simultaneously gaining life from him. And even a little further complicated, perhaps. The ancient word "Eve", the name Adam gave to his new mate, is also the word for "life".'

Both travellers stopped, as if to consider the implications of all of this. But there was another reason for them to pause. Two reasons, in fact. They were now at the edge of the first town – or, realistically, little more than a village – that they had come to. And they were both hungry. Though Scientus seemed as if eager to continue.

'My friend,' Scriptus spoke up first, 'I have muchly enjoyed your company and our morning's discussion. Before we part – although I sincerely hope not for the last time – would you care to join me first for a bite to eat, something to drink perhaps?'

Indeed, they had come to a stop right outside the Emmaus Bakery and Café with its motto emblazoned across the front: "While man might not live on bread alone – you still can't beat a good loaf."

'Delighted,' Scientus replied. 'As your ancient friends might have said, let us break bread together.'